Sing, a Hermit Thrush

ALSO BY
Richard G. Green

The Last Raven and Other Stories

Sing, like a Hermit Thrush

Richard G. Green

Ohsweken

Registered Kanienkehaka Kanonhsyon:ni November 1995
(Julian Calendar)

Ricara Features, Grand River Territory, P.O. Box 269, Ohsweken, Ontario, Canada, NOA 1M0

Ricara Features, via Tuscarora Nation, P.O. Box 664, Sanborn, New York, U.S.A., 14132-0664

All characters, localities, North American Indian Nations and names are used fictitiously or are the product of the author's imagination. Any resemblance to actual localities, events, prophesies and persons living or in the Spirit World is coincidental.

First printed in North America, December, 1995
Soft cover ISBN 0-911737-01-4

acknowledgments

The author wishes to mention several people who helped with this book. They were
all kind enough to read the original manu-
script and offer numerous helpful sugges-
tions, many of which were incorporated in
the final draft. They are: Diane Longboat,
Paul Williams, Anne Thomas, Michael Dox-
tater and Kerri Green.
Nyawen's are also in order for Brian Ma-
racle and Ray Skye who participated in
language clarification and cover realization.
If any errors or implausibilities remain in this
work, the fault is mine.

R.G.G.

ohenton

In general, the following rules apply to English letters:

k=*g*, r=*l*, t=*d*

Mohawk vowels=*English sound like*

a=*aw*, e=*eh*, i=*ee*, o=*o*, en=*en*, on=*own*

First Used Mohawk spelling *English meaning* (actual)

ohenton=*in front of*

Chapter 2: Se:kon=*Hi, hello* (Still? or yet? or again?)

Totah=*Grandparent*

Chapter 3: o'tah=*excrement*

Sekon-Darrin=*to continue on Darrin*

nyawen=*thanks, thank-you*

onenkiwahi=*goodbye*

Chapter 4: ahki=*ouch*

Chapter 5: otkon=*devil*

hanyon oksa=*hurry up*

Chapter 6: atohwitshera=*the Society of Faces*

orenda=*spiritual power*

yokennoron=*It's raining*

yoronhyoron tahnon tetyokarahs=*It's cloudy and dark*

yokennoron yah tewenhniseriyo=*It's raining, it's not a nice day.*

onkwehonwe=*New World Indians* (Turtle Island peoples)

Chapter 7: ah'tso=*brrrr*

nikahneka'a=*the Little Water ceremony*

atohwi=*medicine face mask* (Spirits)

Chapter 9: sataweyat=*you come in*

satyen enitskwara'tsherake=*sit on the chair*

oh nahoten yesayats?=*what is your name?*

Darrin ne yonkyats=*my name is Darrin*

tsi'tenha kiken=*this is a bird*

waton tweet, tweet=*it says tweet, tweet*

sanahskwayen ken nise tsi'tenha?=*do you have a bird?*

toka=*I don't know*

tyohrhenhsa=*English* (language)

sanonhwaktani ken?=*are you sick?*

satonhkaryaks ken?=*are you hungry?*

wakenya tathens=*I'm thirsty*

oh nahoten kiken?=*what is this?*

ohnekawisto=*cold water*

yohnekano=*the water is cold*

ta ne'kati=*it is, so then*

Chapter 11: kahstowa=*Iroquois headdress*

Rotinonhsonni=*the People of the Iroquois longhouse*

"Purify the very breath you breathe with thoughts of the spirit until your thoughts rise like the eagles into the sky, up and up to be one with the Sun and the One who is behind the Sun."

—Tashunka Witko (Crazy Horse)
Lakota Wichasha Wakan

contents

enska (1)

The Strange Dream

"I'm gonna get him."

"What are you looking at?" Darrin looked up into the tree where his friend seemed to be staring.

"He's up there behind that leaf. I'm gonna fire at the leaf and plunk him right off his branch."

"Cut it out Billy." Darrin reached into the pocket of his jeans. "You know you're not supposed to harm any birds." He held up his lucky rabbit's foot by its key-chain then dangled it in Billy's face as if to put a curse on his next shot. "Let's finish the game *if* you can."

Billy reached down, grabbed a steel marble from the circle and stood up. He sighted his target, cocked his arm, wound up as if a Blue Jay's pitcher and let it fly.

Darrin stood up and saw a flash from the steely. He heard it strike a leaf and hit something. Then it fell to the ground with a thud. A second later something else fell to the ground.

"I got him. Just call me a future major leaguer."

The two boys ran over to where a little bird lay. There wasn't any blood and it seemed to be okay. Darrin knelt down and swung his rabbit's foot in a circular motion over the body. He gently picked up the bird while sliding the rabbit's foot back into his pocket. "Sparrow," he said quietly.

Billy picked up the steely. "Is it dead?" He fell to his knees and cleared his throat. "I really didn't mean to..."

Darrin looked at the bird's half-closed eye. Suddenly, everything seemed to go foggy. He squinted at Billy, zoomed in and tried to focus. Instead, Billy dissolved into a flock of birds. Some perched in white trees while others hopped about on fluffy, white earth. Darrin blinked his eyes in amazement but it didn't help. The only things that weren't white were birds!

There were Hawks, Canada Geese, Ducks, and Crows. Darrin recognized Chickadees, Killdeers, Woodpeckers, Gulls, Blue Jays, Robins and Bluebirds. They had all formed into groups and seemed to be arguing among themselves. Each spoke their own language, yet all seemed able to understand each other.

From the Hawk group, a Kestrel, not much bigger than a jay strutted forward. *Killy killy killy* it screeched in a high, excited cry. Then it flew off and went straight up into the sky.

All the birds watched. Some opened their beaks as if amazed at the speck that grew smaller and smaller and smaller. One of the Hawks started to strut but then looked up in surprise. The Kestrel was falling back to earth and it seemed knocked out!

The birds watched in horror as Kestrel plunged straight down. Just before it hit the ground it spread its wings and softened the crash. It skidded to a stop and lay on its belly gasping for breath.

Undaunted, a Red-tailed Hawk stepped forward. It spread its wings, squealed a loud *keeer-r-r* and flew up into the sky. The Kestrel regained its breath, hopped to its feet and smoothed some feathers. He watched his brother Hawk flying higher and higher and higher.

Darrin tried to talk to one of the Geese. Herrmmff-herrmmff is all that came out. He wasn't sure what the birds were doing. Whatever it was, nobody paid any attention to him. Maybe he was invisible. Yeah, that must be it.

The birds groaned disappointment when Red-tailed Hawk returned. It didn't crash; it seemed embarrassed. It gasped for air and hopped behind a tree until everybody focused on another flyer.

All the groups sent a bird to the centre area. A Woodpecker with a zebra-striped back said: *churr churr chiv.* A long-legged Heron pumped out a deep, *oong-ka-choonk, oong-ka-choonk, oong-ka-choonk* song. *Qua-qua-qua*, a duck seemed to laugh. A Killdeer strutted forward and protested *kill-dee, kill-deeee*.

Darrin wondered what they were discussing. He thought he recognized a Chickadee except this one looked different. It had a black line of feathers through its eye and a short tail. Instead of a *chick-a-dee-dee-dee-dee* song it uttered a more nasal *enk*.

Just as it seemed to be saying *enk*, a crow uttered its *caw-caw* call. Darrin heard enk-caw and puzzled over its meaning. He remembered the dancers that he met at a powwow. They said they were Inca Indians, but did *enk-caw* mean Inca?

He also knew that in his mother tongue, Mohawk, enska meant one. It must be *en* instead of *in* he thought. Yes, they must be saying *enska*. But why the number one?

A brown, black-necked Goose strode forward. Darrin guessed it to be leader of the geese because it was bigger than the rest. As it waddled toward the middle of the circle, an all-white Swan also went there. They both looked mean and stared at each other beak to beak. Darrin expected them to fight.

Instead, they jumped up and beat their wings. Seven-foot wing spans churned the air and kicked up dust. Some of the smaller birds twittered and chirped. *Caw-caw*, a crow scolded.

They lifted off and flew higher and higher until

they disappeared into the clouds. *Qua-qua-qua* said the ducks as if to cheer their cousins on.

Suddenly, a big shadow spread over the ground. It caused all the birds to shut up and take notice. *Squeeeee-e-e* came a loud screech from above. *Squee-ee-e-e.* All the birds watched as mighty Eagle feathered his wings and lit on top of a tall, white pine tree.

Everybody heard a faint whistling sound and a squeaking *honk-honk-honk.* The Swan and Goose were returning. But instead of flying, it looked as if they were falling! When they got closer, they seemed barely able to flap their wings to avoid crashing to the ground. The Swan's beak was open while it gasped for air and the Goose bounced twice when it landed.

Darrin wanted to help in some way but there was nothing he could do. The Swan had landed safely. It lowered its long neck as if shamed when it went back to its place outside the circle. When the Goose finally stood up and fluffed its feathers, Darrin felt better. It slowly waddled over and stood beside the Swan. *Qua-qua-qua-qua ,* said the ducks.

A sudden movement caught the corner of Darrin's eye. He heard the whoosh and mighty wing beats of Eagle as it landed in the centre of the circle. Eagle walked around looking at all the birds like a commander inspecting his troops. With mean-looking Eagle eyes he stared at the birds of prey, hopped past the wading birds and cast a craving glance at the plump, fowl-like birds.

As he turned to take off, a small bird sneaked out from under the branches of the pine tree and hopped upon his back. Eagle looked around but the little bird had burrowed beneath his tail feathers. Nobody said anything. Eagle jumped into the air, flapped his giant, eight-foot wings and took off. The little brown bird hung on tightly as they went up and up. They soared in great circles, riding thermal air currents until they were out of sight.

A hush fell over the anxious crowd while they waited. Some started to pace. Swan and Goose seemed fully recovered but stayed out of Darrin's sight. They were beat and everybody left them alone.

When the first *squeeeee-e-e-e* sounded, everybody looked skyward. Eagle hurtled toward the ground. His hooked beak lay open catching as much air as it could and his glazed eyes were half closed. He swooped and landed with a thud but his great talons dug in and held him erect.

Darrin wondered about the little bird with the rusty tail. Had it fallen off his back? Had Eagle got angry or hungry and eaten him?

"Hey Darrin!"

Darrin felt himself being shook.

"Let him go," Billy said. "You're holding on to him too

tightly. I don't want you to kill him, okay?"

Darrin looked into Billy's concerned face. He felt the Sparrow squirm in his hand. "Billy?"

"He's all right, must'ta just been stunned. Let him go, okay?"

Darrin felt the bird's heart pounding so hard it seemed ready to explode. When he opened his hand, the Sparrow blinked and quickly flew into a big chestnut tree.

"Wow...did you see that?" Darrin said. He couldn't believe what had just happened to him.

"Of course I saw that."

"I don't mean the Sparrow. I mean all those other birds."

"What birds?" Billy knelt down. "There's only one bird just like there's only one marble."

"No, no. All the birds that were in that white place." Darrin sank to his knees. "Didn't you see them?"

"What white place?" Billy carefully aimed at the only marble left in the circle. "You going crazy, man?" He flipped his steely and knocked it out. "Well, that's all for today." He picked it up and dropped it into his pocket. "Unless you got more marbles stashed away in your sister's house."

Darrin's thoughts weren't on marbles or Billy. He said nothing when Billy hopped on his skateboard, played catch with the steely and pushed himself off down the street. He didn't even answer when Billy yelled "Later!"

Instead, Darrin wondered about the little brown bird and what might have become of it. Yet something drew him toward the house and he sprang up the porch steps. He noticed L. Lafont printed on the mailbox of the owner's house. He wondered why his sister and her live-with man didn't have one.

He felt the rabbit foot in his pocket getting warm. He threw open the screen door and bolted upstairs to the second floor. He tried jumping two stairs at a time, stumbled, caught himself and continued.

The little brown bird with the rusty-coloured tail would have to wait for now. Darrin felt an emergency coming on.

tekeni (2)

The Accurate Prediction

He tripped over the top step and fell against the kitchen door with a thud. He caught the doorknob, twisted it and burst inside.

"Lisa!" he yelled to his sister. "Have you got a bandage in this house?"

"Chill-out, will ya," Lisa said. "You'll have to get it yourself, I'm giving the baby a bath, eh?"

While bent over the sink, she held the baby's head up with one hand and scooped water over it with the other. Darrin's nose filled with baby smells. A calmness swept over him when he saw baby Naomi's wide-set brown eyes.

"They're right in there," Lisa motioned with her chin toward a drawer. "But first, pull my hair back will you? I don't want it to get into Naomi's bath water."

Darrin's thoughts turned to his rabbit's foot. He wondered how it could get warm all by itself. It never got really hot, just rather warm. Every time it did, something always seemed to happen. Like now.

"Earth to Darrin, pay attention will ya? What did you skin this time, your elbow or your knee?"

Darrin carefully gathered Lisa's long, black hair. "I didn't skin nothing," he said. "Old Man Lafont just stuck himself on a thorn." He tucked hair behind her ears and draped some of it over her slender shoulders. "He'll probably *bleed* to death without one."

"Okay, go ahead and take him one. But stay around the house. Mark will be home any minute now and I don't want to spend all day looking for you."

Darrin pulled the drawer open, removed a bandage from its package and pushed it closed. Adults just couldn't rest until they told you what to do. No way could he be left behind. Today was Saturday and he couldn't miss ball practice or he'd be off the team.

He bolted from the kitchen, hopped upon the banister and slid to the bottom of the stairs. He burst from the screen door, jumped off the porch and raced down the driveway into the backyard. An old man wearing a straw hat and suspenders knelt beside a rose bush.

"Se:kon, Mr. Lafont," Darrin said.

Mr. Lafont carefully worked his pruning shears. He spit out some tobacco and his big ears made his hat move as he chewed it. He had a small chin and skin hung from his neck in folds.

Darrin wondered if Mr. Lafont heard him. "Hello, Mr. Lafont," he repeated.

Suddenly, Mr. Lafont flinched. "Ouch!" he dropped the shears and a drop of blood squeezed from his finger. "Damn-it," he said. "Oh, hello Darrin." He sucked on the finger.

"I've got this bandage for you." Darrin proudly held it out.

Mr. Lafont looked at his bloody finger. "Well aren't you Johnny-on-the-spot. Look at this thing bleed, will you." Mr. Lafont put his finger back in his mouth.

Darrin wondered how much money Mr. Lafont would give him this time. Sometimes, on a good day, he coughed up paper money. Since he got stuck with a thorn, Darrin figured he'd probably only be good for a loonie today. He waved the bandage to make sure the old man saw it.

Mr. Lafont grabbed it, pulled his finger from his mouth and quickly wound his finger. "How'd you know I'd be needing this?" he said.

Darrin shrugged and looked down. "Sometimes I know things," he stammered. He wanted to tell somebody about how his rabbit's foot got warm and how he could feel other things too. Natural stuff like who was going to get born and when it would lightning.

"Tell ya what I really need, kid." Mr. Lafont's cheek's puffed out from the wad of chewing tobacco. "I want to water these here roses tomorrah and I need a little rain." He spat out some tobacco goo. "Why don't you do a little rain dance for me?"

Darrin guessed he was kidding because he smiled when he said it. He wondered if Mr. Lafont really thought some Indians were dancing someplace every time it rained.

"No, I can't dance today...I don't have the proper attire..."

"Fire? Did you say fire?"

"No, attire." Darrin raised his voice. "You know, clothes."

"Why d'ya want to dance in your clothes? Looks a lot better when you Indians dance in your costumes."

From behind, Darrin heard a window slide open. Mrs. Lafont thrust her head out. Her shiny, white hair had roots that had turned the colour of mold.

"LawrENCE LAFont," her voice cracked. "You knOW IT'S LUNChtime!" She jerked her head inside and slammed the window shut. A chunk of putty fell out.

Mr. Lafont stood up, aimed at the rose bush and spat at its roots. "Damn woman," he snorted. "Man cain't never get no work done 'round here." He threw down the shears, reached into a baggy pocket in his corduroy pants and pulled out a loonie. "Here kid." He flipped it high in the air and trudged toward the back door.

Darrin missed the dollar coin. It flipped on its edge and rolled down the driveway. He stepped on it and picked it up. He put it in his pocket and bolted toward the front porch. Half-way down the driveway, he heard a familiar brake-squeal sound. Mark had just parked his new car in front of the house.

Darrin decided to hide and leaned back against the wall. With arms outstretched, he carefully slid along the house to the backyard. Mark hadn't seen him; he sighed and slid to a sitting position.

Darrin figured it was always better to leave adults alone when they were working. Poor ole redheaded Mark would have to load up the car with Naomi's car seat and baby junk. Then he'd have to load up Lisa's junk. There just wasn't any point in getting in their way.

If they want me, he mused, they'll call out. When you got in their way, you always got the ole Eagle-eye look. Like the time he had predicted Naomi's birth...

That night, Darrin's parents left him with Aunty Julie. It got late so Darrin went to sleep on her couch. Suddenly, the phone rang and Darrin heard Aunty Julie say: "Oh, it's a girl named Naomi which weighs 7 pounds and 2 ounces. Mother Lisa and baby Naomi are doing just fine." Aunt Julie hung up the phone. Darrin remembered sitting up. He looked at the digital clock and it read 4:15 AM.

Later during the ride home, Darrin's father speculated about his sister's progress in hospital. He wanted to know if her baby would be a girl or a boy. When Darrin told him Naomi was a 7 pound, 2 ounce girl and everything at the hospital turned out fine, he couldn't believe it.

"How do you know?" Mum asked him.

"Because somebody phoned and told Aunty Julie. I seen it."

"You must have made a mistake." Darrin's dad took one hand off the steering wheel. "I asked her about it when we came to pick you up. She said she hadn't heard anything yet." He faced Darrin and gave off the ole Eagle-eye right through the darkness.

Even though Darrin knew he was right, he didn't argue. He hated it when adults didn't believe him about stuff. This time, he hated it even more because it was his own mum and dad.

Next morning, Darrin's parents woke up by a phone call from Mark. He told them Naomi was born at 4:15 AM and Lisa was okay. When they called to tell Aunty Julie, they found out that she didn't know anything about Naomi's birth until they told her. No, she hadn't received any phone calls while Darrin slept on the couch.

Suddenly, Darrin heard the *clak-clak-clak* of footsteps coming from the driveway. Mark was the only person he knew that walked with a soldier's precision. He pushed himself up into a standing position and shaded his eyes.

"Dar-RIN!" Mark yelled. "You're holding us up!"

Darrin knew that timing was key in this situation. If he went to them too soon, they'd get mad because he made them yell. Adults don't like to yell. So the trick is to let them think you're lost. Let them think about spending the whole day searching for you. Then when you pop out they're glad to see you.

He waited until Mark went down the block yelling his name. When he came back again, Darrin hopped out from around the corner of the house. He watched Mark's frown turn into a relieved look.

"Oh good," Mark said. "There you are little brother." He reached for Darrin's hand. "Come on..."

"I'm not your brother!" Darrin squirted past him and ran to the car. "Lisa!" He got in and slammed the door. "Keep your husband away from me."

Darrin slouched down in the back seat. He wondered why he went rather crazy in the city sometimes. He didn't dislike Mark but something about the guy just wasn't right. Besides, these vision things seemed to be happening more frequently. They were getting out of hand. He'd have to tell somebody. He'd have to get help.

In that case, he'd prefer going home to Totah's and

telling good ole Fox. Yeah, Fox. He'd know just what to do. He felt relieved when the car pulled away from Lisa's apartment.

ahsen (3)

One Sorry Bull

Darrin liked the leather smell inside Mark's new car. So when they pulled off the highway and Mark went inside Cobe's Gas Bar to buy groceries he sat and sniffed the seats.

Going shopping with Mark made no sense anyway. Mark always took food with him when he went to the Rez, but he seldom bought anything Darrin suggested. Like candy or sugar-coated breakfast cereal.

"Yechhh..." Darrin wrinkled his nose. "Did Naomi just load her pants?"

"'Fraid so," said Lisa. She laid Naomi on a blanket and began unwrapping a smelly diaper.

"I'm gonna go and check out the magazine rack."

"Take this and put it in the garbage barrel over there." Lisa handed him the smelly diaper. "Here," she motioned. "It won't kill you, you know."

"Yechhh. O'tah will get *on* me."

"It won't get on you. I folded it up."

Darrin dodged between gas pumps. He slam-dunked the diaper into the barrel and noticed a sign in the window. He stopped and read: PART-TIME HELP WANTED. He guessed Mark would apply for the job. Mark liked to work. He liked money and bought expensive things for himself and sometimes for Lisa too.

"Sekon-Darrin," came a voice from behind. "Do you s'pose I could get a ride home with you?"

Darrin recognized Dale Joshua, one of his classmates. "I dunno." He pushed the screen door open. "It's my sister's husband's car. I'll try to ask." Darrin went inside and the door slapped shut.

Cobe's was a shabby little place packed with supplies. Adults could get stuff for nothing one day and pay money to Mr. Cobe another day. Darrin even tried it once. That's when he realized how much adults stick together. Mr. Cobe told him credit is for adults only.

He went straight to the magazine rack, picked up *Dirt Bike* and started looking at its pictures. He saw a dusty, blue pick-up truck pull in and park. Arley Van Peldt vaulted from its bed. He scraped manure from the heel of his work boots and lumbered inside. Two pimples rode above his thin, seagull lips. He pushed past Darrin and grabbed a copy of *Playboy*. Turning his back as if to avoid Mr. Cobe, he dropped open the centrefold.

"Hey Darrin," he said. "Get a look at this beaver." He nudged Darrin's shoulder with his elbow.

Darrin nodded and turned away. He wondered what a Beaver would be doing in a magazine full of naked girls.

"Heyyy. Don't turn away from me! What's the matter? Don't you like looking at bare-naked white women?" His eyes narrowed into slits. "When I show you something, you look. Get it?"

Darrin felt his knees go weak. He remembered Arley was two years older and used to be his best friend. He even told him about one of his visions, but Arley only laughed. Darrin figured Arley must be turning into an adult. Probably that's why he's turning so nasty.

Suddenly he felt the centrefold being crushed into his face. He pushed away and the magazine fell to the floor. "What are you doing?" he gasped.

"I saw you throw that magazine on the floor," Arley snorted. "Now pick it up!"

Darrin looked into a pair of steely-eyes. "I, I never did," he gulped. "*You* did." His insides felt soft as a jelly doughnut. Suddenly, he heard something crumple.

"Here, let's go little brother." Mark thrust a grocery bag into Darrin's arms. Stepping over the centrefold, he put an arm around Darrin's shoulder and guided him outside. "You shouldn't be looking at that stuff anyway," he said.

"I wasn't looking at anything..."

Mark smiled. "Right," he said. "You've got plenty of time to worry about women when you grow up."

Darrin looked into the bag but instead of candy, cake or pop he saw toilet paper. He wanted to tell Mark that at Totah's they always use newspaper in the outhouse. He figured Mark wouldn't believe him anyway. Still, he had to be kind to him. After all, he just saved his life.

"Totah, uh, Grandpa'll like this pink toilet paper," he lied. He knew Totah would never use it.

In the excitement, Darrin forgot to ask about taking another passenger. With two big bags of toilet paper, milk and baby food, there wouldn't be enough room anyway. So he pretended not to see Dale Joshua as they climbed into Mark's car and drove away. When he peeked back, he saw Arley reach out and pull Dale up into the bed of the blue pick-up.

They turned off the main highway to a narrower, two-lane road. Though a longer route to the reserve, it had fewer gravelled roads. Tidy farms graced the rolling countryside and stiff barnyard odours flooded the car. Mark closed his window. Naomi, wrapped like a mummy in pink blankets, seemed content to wave her arms and slobber.

"You know," Mark said to Lisa. "I'm not going to miss living at the Lafont's apartment. But I am going to miss the cheap rent. If we had waited to have children like I wanted, we wouldn't have to move now."

"You know I don't believe in planning, Mark. The Creator decides when things get born, not people. I told you what to expect before we got together."

"Yes, I know, but this is..."

Darrin squirmed. He didn't like arguments so he shut off their conversation. He watched familiar bends in the olive-coloured river speed by his window. They were on the reserve now and the houses were closer together.

"Darrin...Darrin!"

Darrin saw Mark staring at him through the rear view mirror. "And that's what you should be thinking about, little brother," he said. "Planning what you're going to be doing with your life." He turned the steering wheel and they went down a gravelled road. "Decide on a goal and start working toward it. That job back there at Cobe's would be an excellent start."

Darrin pushed his window button down and took a deep breath. He heard wind noise and felt it pushing against his hair. Here I am, he thought, barely out of school for the summer and Mark expects me to begin working. No way can I take that job. It's way too far for a bicycle commute. Heck-enit, it's even a half-hour by car.

"I don't have anyone to drive me," he said.

A sense of freedom welled up inside and when they passed Sharla Whitepine's house he knew they'd soon be at Totah's. Turning the corner, he recognized his old school. It felt good to be around familiar things. It felt good to be back home on the Rez.

"There's my ole school," Darrin said proudly.

"You're all finished there now, aren't you?"

"Yeah. I'll have to take the bus into town, next year. I'd rather stay here but we got no High School."

They turned and went between two oak trees. They followed a tire pathway toward a two-story, Insul-brick house. Its narrow end faced the road and you couldn't tell its size until you circled a basswood tree and stopped beside it. Darrin looked for Totah's old Ford but couldn't see it anywhere.

Cousin Brenda waved from inside the house. When the car stopped, Darrin grabbed two bags filled with toilet paper and ran inside. A stale aroma of split wood came from the wood box. Kerosene smells from two lamps made his nose wrinkle as he placed the bags upon the kitchen table.

"Se:kon. Se:kon-Darrin," Brenda said.

Her thick glasses made her green eyes appear cross-eyed. But Darrin knew better. He knew that like all adults, she could see things that weren't there.

"Se:kon," he said.

"How was your visit?"

Before Darrin could answer, Lisa came in with Naomi. Brenda quickly took the baby and pinched Mark's waist when he came through the door. "You've got to put some weight on this guy, Lisa," she said. "Enit Darrin?" She winked. "Good wind storm and you'll be lookin' for another man."

"Nah," Lisa smiled. "There's enough of him to put up with all ready."

"Well, don't just stand there," Brenda said to Darrin. "Go get some wood for the stove and make fire. I've got to boil water for tea. There's some corn soup left if you want to eat before you go to ball practice."

Darrin scampered to the wood box. He carefully selected three logs and put them on top of the iron stove. He glanced at an empty nail where the lid-handle hung. "Where's the handle?" He looked at Brenda. "I can't make a fire without it."

"It got lost but don't let that stop you. Put the logs in the bottom. You'll have to take the ashes out first." She jiggled Naomi. "The scoop's on the other side, there."

She gently slid her palm over Naomi's forehead and began unwrapping her. In baby talk she said, "It's too warm for all these covers." She handed the blanket to Mark. "There, that's better, enit Naomi?"

She handed the baby to Lisa and took an apron from a drawer. "Darrin! Get some water from the well...and don't fall in!"

Darrin cleaned ashes from the stove and made a pile behind the house. He lit the fire, grabbed a pail and ran past Brenda's flower garden toward the well.

It took him three tries to properly tip the pail and fill it with water. On his way back to the house, a garter snake wriggled near his foot and he spilled water on his pants. Horses neighed at him from the barn where Fox usually hung out.

He hopped up on the high step, opened the door and placed the pail on its stand. "Is Fox out in the barn?" He reached under the stove for the dish pan.

"No. He went with Larry-Jam to get some guitar strings," Brenda said. "They're playing at the Hall for a wedding dance tonight. Ross went with Totah to get some bread and milk."

"How long ago did they leave?" Darrin put some water in the pan.

"Little over an hour ago."

"I gotta see Fox right now. When will he be home?"

"Not a minute before he gets here," laughed Brenda. "Hey! Don't spill any water on my clean floor."

"Can I go tonight?"

"Little impatient, are we now?" Brenda's face looked smug. "I happen to know that you don't want to go to the dance just to see Fox. You want to go to see your cute little girlfriend."

"*Girl*friend?"

"Yes, girlfriend. I know all about Sharla Whitepine. She came here with her brother to pick you up. She wants to go to ball practice with you."

Darrin figured all adults must be goofy. When somebody wanted to go to ball practice with you it didn't mean anything. Besides, Sharla was taller than him; he only came up to her nose. Not that he minded her. She always had a smile for everybody and seemed like a pleasant kid. And if he went with Sharla, he wouldn't have to beg a ride from Mark.

After they ate, Darrin bounded upstairs. Thoughts of Arley crowded Sharla from his mind. He changed his clothes making sure he put on his best Blue Jay's T-shirt. The one that said World Champions. He figured that if Arley started up with him at ball practice, he'd need all the help he could get. He wished he could make Arley twitch. Sometimes, wishing very hard worked. Like the time he got even with a mean ole bull...

That day, because of a thunderstorm, he had taken a shortcut home. He climbed over a rail fence and gingerly went through a cow pasture. He knew that a mean ole bull lived there. He made sure not to throw stones at any of the cows. He was almost half-way across when he heard a snort.

The bull saw him and charged. Darrin turned and ran for the fence as fast as he could. He heard pounding hoof-beats behind him. He felt the bull's hot breath on his neck. He dove under the bottom rail just in time. He landed face-first in a puddle of cow dung.

Darrin caught rain in his hands and wiped off his face. He squeezed dung out of his hair. He watched the joyful bull trot back to his cows. All of them mooed at him. Then they turned around and mooned him. Darrin wished as hard as he could that the tree beside the bull would get hit by lightning.

Sssbrunnng!

An oak branch split and uttered a loud groan. The bull looked up and his big eyes turned white with fear. Foam came from his mouth, his ears swept back and he started to buck. He bucked and bucked and bucked until he fell over from exhaustion. Raindrops made steam rise from his hot body. Though Darrin got soaking wet, it felt good to get even with the bull. Even if the poor tree had to lose one of its arms.

He wondered if wishing could work again? He remembered those genie books where you get three wishes. If true, it meant that he still had two left. He could use one on Arley to make him twitch. He could use the last one to wish for three more wishes. But what if Arley kept twitching for the rest of his life? He didn't want that to happen.

"I'm not going to ball practice today," he yelled toward the stairwell for somebody to hear. He kicked his softball glove under the bed and waited. "I can't find my glove."

He went to the window to watch a wasp and saw Sharla hop out of a sleek car. Wind blew her silken hair into the corner of her mouth and she tilted her head upward. She saw Darrin, gave a cheerful smile and waved. Her lips read: "Come on."

Darrin grabbed the glove from under his bed and bounded down stairs. Who knows? Arley might not even show up at ball practice.

During the drive to the fairgrounds Sharla barely spoke. Even when she did, her brother only grunted his answer. She must be intimidated by him, Darrin thought. That's why she isn't talking to me. Yeah, that's it. Still, you'd think that somebody who's madly in love with you could find something to say.

"I saw a big snake by our well today," Darrin said to get the ball rolling.

"I hate snakes." Sharla looked out her window.

Nothing else was said during the whole trip. They came into the village, drove by the fairground's gatehouse and parked next to a white, racetrack fence.

Darrin grabbed his glove, threw open the door and hopped outside. "Nyawen for the ride," he said. "See you after...onenkiwahi."

He wasted little time running across the dusty race track to the ball diamond. Whew, he said under his breath. To think I almost bought Sharla some chips with my loonie. He thumped his fist into his glove.

He couldn't help but notice the arrival of Arley Van Peldt and Dale Joshua. They vaulted over the racetrack rail in unison, agile as two whitetail Deer. They moved to centre field with strides sure as a pair of Clydesdales. Dale carried their ball gloves.

Arley looked toward Darrin. He had a toothpick in the corner of his mouth but said nothing. For now at least, he kept his fingers tucked into the slash pockets of his jeans.

kayeri (4)

The Arley Run-in

They alternated catching fly balls. Every time the coach hit one over Arley's head, Dale chased it. Coach called the players together and made them line up. When he picked teams for a game, they sat down on the dugout bench. They didn't need to worry about making the team. They were its battery: Arley pitched and Dale caught.

Sharla and her brother sat down behind the home plate screen. Arley noticed. He took off his glove and threw it in the air as if trying to get her attention. When he did, he pushed out his lips and twirled his toothpick. This action made Sharla blush.

"Captain over here," Coach motioned with his clipboard.

Darrin leaped forward.

"Not you, Captain. The team's captain." Coach shaded his eyes. "Arley, where are you?"

Darrin faced a sea of snickering faces. He hoped Sharla hadn't seen his goof but realized she did. His eyes lowered to the dirt as he trudged back in line with the other fidgeting players.

Arley stepped forward. "You want me to start the game today, Coach, or finish up?"

Coach pushed the visor of his cap up with his pencil. "Uh, you can finish up. I want to try something. Why don't you sit down for a while and rest up." He pointed his pencil toward Darrin. "I want you to play second today, Darrin. You know how to play second base don't you?"

"Yeah Coach," Darrin nodded and trotted out to his position. What else could he say in front of Sharla and the whole world? He hated playing second base because nobody taught him how to make a double-play pivot. But he liked it better than centre field. He worried that he couldn't throw the ball far enough to play that position. Arley intentionally brushed against him on his way to the bench.

"We're only playing five innings today," Coach announced. "I've got a meeting with a possible sponsor and I've got to go." Coach walked toward the bench. "Arley? You sit out the first two innings and then come in."

Darrin kicked at some pebbles. He'd seen second baseman do that on TV. He had tried out to play right field. Nobody ever hit the ball there. In right, he could play shallow and reach home with his weak throwing arm. He wished he had practised throwing. He wished he had those iron weights to lift like on TV. Then his arm would be strong enough.

Last year, he didn't even make the team. Everybody always told him not to worry; he'd get better next year. Now, it was next year and he still wasn't better. Now, they wanted him to play crummy ole second base. He reasoned that when adults can't find a good answer they always say: wait until next year.

During the practice game, Darrin lucked-out. Nobody had hit the ball to him; he had no chances. He even spun one off the end of his bat and ran to first for a base hit. He heard Sharla say: "Way to go Darrin" and he thought about stealing second. That would really impress her. Arley had come in to pitch in the third inning.

In the top half of the fourth, Coach pulled the pencil from behind his ear. He handed his clipboard to the University kid who served as umpire. As Darrin watched Coach leaving, he felt a tingling begin in his toes. A kind of electricity began energizing him and shot up into his legs. He knew something was going to happen. Too bad Coach wouldn't see him humble Arley's team.

In the top of the fifth, after they batted, Arley's team

stayed around their dugout bench. Instead of taking the field, they started goofing off. They always fooled around whenever Coach wasn't there to see them. Arley gave Dale his glove to carry and other players started gathering up their equipment. They were going to leave with a 12-10 victory.

Darrin and his team-mates hustled toward their bench eager for their last at-bats. Darrin saw Sharla standing behind the backstop. She stood next to her brother with a puzzled look on her kitten-like face.

"Where do you guys think you're going!" Darrin yelled. "We have to play five *full* innings!" He looked at the University kid umpire. "Coach said!"

The University kid looked at his wrist watch. "We've got the field for fifteen more minutes." He dusted off home plate with three sweeps of his sneakers. "Play ball! Arley, get your team out there." He threw Arley the ball. "Let's go. Let's get a better up there!"

Arley glared at Darrin as his team grudgingly took their positions. "Don't worry guys," he snorted. "I'll get 'em one-two-three!"

True to his word, he struck out the first two batters. Needing only one more out, he started to fool around. He threw some experimental pitches that bounced on top of the plate. Even Dale showed disgust when Arley walked the next two batters. He went out to the rubber to talk things over.

Darrin carefully selected three bats and started swinging them. One of them slipped out of his grip and fell on his foot. Ahki! He selected a blue one and looked toward Sharla. Her fingers were dangerously wrapped around the backstop screen. A foul tip could break them but Darrin knew there wouldn't be any foul tips.

Arley glared at Darrin. Then Dale turned to look at him. They both laughed as Dale trotted back to his position behind the plate.

"Come on Darrin!" Sharla's brother cupped his hands into a megaphone. "Hit a home run for Sharla."

Darrin heard Sharla giggle. He stepped up to the plate and tapped his sneakers with the aluminium bat. A puff of wind blew dust in his eye. He tried washing it away by blinking. Arley's first pitch sailed in.

"Steee-one!" the University kid yelled.

Darrin stepped out of the batter's box. He rested the bat against his leg, raised his arm and wiped his eye with his sleeve. He grabbed the bat, stepped up to the plate and dug in. With his head down and the bat resting on his shoulder, the next pitch buzzed past.

"Steee-two."

"Come on, Arley," Dale shouted. "No stick! No stick!"

Arley smiled. "I oughtta waste the next one and put it right down his throat."

Darrin smiled at the University kid. He flashed a sly

smile to Sharla. He pointed the bat over Arley's head toward centre field. The next pitch sailed in.

WHOPP!

Arley threw himself to the ground as the ball zoomed past his head. Then it went up, up, up, far out into centre field. Darrin took off fast as he could. The ball bounced off the fence and the fielder threw it in. Darrin sped around third base. The cut-off man turned and fired it home. Darrin dove for the plate. He touched it with his finger just as Dale slapped the big catchers' mitt on his head.

"Safe!" shouted the University kid. "Games over." He looked at Darrin. "You win 13-12."

"Shit," said Dale. "He was out! I had him by three feet!"

Darrin got up and dusted himself off. He felt his hair being mussed up by happy team-mates. One of them gave him high and low fives. He walked toward the backstop wondering if Sharla saw what happened. He saw her brother walking toward them eating from a box of french fries.

"That was cool," Sharla flashed a smile.

"I knew I could do it," Darrin said quietly. Two guys who were leaving tossed his glove to him.

"Bet you couldn't do that in a real game."

"What do you mean?" Darrin frowned. "This was a real game." He slumped against the fence and punched the pocket of his glove. Suddenly, he felt something push against his shoulder.

"You did that on purpose, didn't you." Arley said. "I saw you point your bat at me."

"And you were out at home plate too," Dale said.

"Was not," Darrin turned to face Arley and Dale. "You heard the ump."

"You almost hit me with the ball." Arley pushed Darrin's chest with his hands. "And on account of you, old man Cole says I can't look at *Playboy* no more."

"Old man Cole?"

"Yeah." Arley pushed Darrin again. "He came over and made me pick up the magazine you threw on the floor. When he saw what it was, he said I can't read it no more."

A shiver ran up Darrin's spine. He straightened his body and looked into Arley's eyes. He concentrated hard as he could. He had decided to make Arley's eyes start twitching. Simultaneously. He knew Arley meant business; his eyes looked fiery as the bull's when it charged him.

Arley turned so that his eyes weren't in the sun. Darrin turned with him and squinted. Suddenly, Arley reared back, placed both hands on his chest and...whoosh! Darrin tumbled over Dale's back and landed in the dust. His glove came off and he reached for it but Dale kicked it away.

A fist crashed against his nose. "Ow!" He tried to put his guard up but felt an explosion above his left eye. Another stung the corner of his mouth. Arley flopped on top of him and started punching his ribs. He twisted his body to squirm loose and the loonie fell out of his pocket. He felt a fist hit the back of his head as Arley straddled him.

"Hey, look what I found," Arley said. He held up the loonie.

Darrin twisted around to see. "That's mine," he said. "You can't have it, it's a gift."

"It sure is." Arley stood up, brushed himself off and winked at Sharla. "Come on Dale." He put his arm around Dale's shoulder. "Let's *vous* and *moi* go get us some pop."

Darrin dabbed his wrist at the corner of his mouth and saw blood. He pushed himself up, slapped dust from his jeans and picked up his glove. He stretched his tongue to the corner of his mouth. He tasted a salty mixture of blood and snivel. So much for trying to make Arley's eyes twitch, he thought.

"Fighting is such a silly, stupid thing," Sharla said. "Why do you boys always have to be fighting, anyway?"

Sharla's brother handed Darrin a napkin. "Be careful. It's got some vinegar on it," he said. "Are you all right?" He inspected Darrin's mouth.

Darrin took a shot at humour. "I wasn't fighting," he said remembering that he didn't get off a single punch. He tried to laugh it off and the corner of his mouth hurt. "Ahki!"

"I'm sorry you got hurt," Sharla said.

"It's nothing," Darrin said. He tried to spit away some of the slobber but it stuck to his lip and spattered his World Champion T-shirt.

A cloud of quiet hung inside the car for the entire trip home. This time, Darrin didn't care because when he tried to talk to Sharla his lip hurt. By the time they pulled up beside Totah's house, his whole face felt stiff as glass. He mumbled a thank you to Sharla, got out and pushed the car door closed. When he put on his glove, his arm felt like a rubber band.

He stood for a while and watched the car leave. He figured Sharla wouldn't want to go with him to ball practice anymore. Girls don't like a wimp.

He walked like a zombie toward the house and hoped Brenda wouldn't be inside. He knew she'd want to know everything that happened but he didn't feel like explaining.

He looked up at the kitchen window. Brenda always watched everybody coming and going. He didn't see her. Good. She wasn't at home.

wisk (5)

Darrin's Decision

Brenda stood near the kitchen table with hands on hips. Darrin tried to pucker his lips and whistle as if nothing had happened. Blips of pain whizzed through his face.

"Otkon!" Brenda moved in for a closer look. "What happened to you?" She pushed her thumb against Darrin's nose.

"Ahki!" Darrin jerked away. "What are you doing?"

"Well at least your nose isn't broken." She guided him into a chair. "Who did this to you?"

"Arley Van Peldt."

"I thought youse were friends." She flashed Darrin the ole eagle-eye. "How come he beat you up?"

Darrin felt his eyes sink to the floor. There, she's got me again, he thought. Whatever I say, she'll say I'm guilty. Tell her about Arley stealing my loonie and she'll want to know where I got it? Tell her about winning the game with my homer and it's my fault for bragging. You don't brag about yourself or it will come back on you. Which lecture do I want to hear? Lecture number one is about not taking money from people. Lecture number two is about not being a braggart.

Darrin chose number two. He didn't want to reveal Mr. Lafont as his secret money source. Maybe he could escape the heat by not saying anything. He decided to study a shiny knot-hole he found in a floorboard.

"Arley's bigger than you, did you get some licks in?"

"Nah," Darrin stammered. "I never even hit him once."

"Well, you know, this'll keep on happening until you either lick him or put up a good fight."

"But he's two years older than me."

"Age don't mean nothing." Brenda reached behind the wood box for the pail. "Even if you lose he won't want to mess with you." She took his glove and handed him the pail. "Get to the well, fill this up, wash the blood off your face and rinse-out your T-shirt. Bring the rest back to the house."

Darrin trudged toward the well. Easy for her to say, he said under his breath. She's an adult. Adults never fight. He drew a pail of water, placed it on the ground and looked at his reflection. He saw a cut above his eyebrow and a flap of lip-skin hanging from the corner of his mouth. Darn that Arley.

He cupped his hands and splashed water against his

face. "Ahki!" His eye stung. He took off his T-shirt, poured water on it and wrung it out. His arms trembled while he scrubbed clots of blood from his chin.

He realized, as usual, that Brenda was right. Adults always seemed to be experts in matters like this. He reached into his pocket and pulled out his rabbit's foot. What good are these vision-things if they don't work when you need them, he thought. I guess I'll have to ask Fox to teach me how to fight. When Fox lived in the Army, he had fights in a real boxing ring.

He slipped the T-shirt over his shoulder and picked up the pail. He could only carry it for ten feet before he stopped to rest. When he got to the clothes' line, he hung his T-shirt over it. He puckered up to whistle but cringes of pain made him stop. He'd have to give up whistling for a while.

He stumbled into the house. "Where's Fox?"

Brenda sat at the table reading a newspaper. "The guys are playing for a wedding dance tonight at the Hall, remember? If you want to go, you'd better get in a clean shirt and comb your hair."

"Where's Mark and Lisa? How are we going to get there without a ride?"

"They went to visit Aunty Julie and show her Mark's new car. We're leaving as soon as they get back." She folded up the paper and put it down. "So you better hurry up. Hanyon oksa! Hanyon oksa!"

Darrin bounded upstairs. Brenda had put a clean T-shirt on his bed and he slipped into it. "Owww!" The neck hole rubbed against his nose and made him wince. "Ahki!"

He reflected that today hadn't been one of his better days. He won the ballgame but still ended up being a wimp. Right in front of Sharla. Darn that Arley.

He guessed that learning the fight game would be easy. He all ready knew how to properly clench his fists. And he didn't want to learn everything, just a few different punches.

Cousin Fox knew all the ropes. He had learned boxing in the army and even turned professional for a while. But Darrin didn't have time to become a professional. He had to take a short cut. He'd only learn the punches he needed to take care of Arley. He figured the whole lesson would take about an hour.

He thought: So Sharla thinks I'm a wimp, eh? Maybe that's a good thing...at least for tonight. He pondered how he might generate some pity from her at the dance. He expected her to be there because everybody on the reserve always went to wedding dances.

Even though he hated being pitied by anyone, Sharla was different. He didn't know exactly when she had become the exception.

yayak (6)

The Wedding Dance

To Darrin's eyes, Community Hall looked like a lake steamer afloat in a parking lot full of cars. Its sky-blue clapboard siding seemed like a water line for its composition brick hull. To the east, a racetrack rail fronted a grandstand and circled the ball diamond where he had knocked his homer.

Inside the old Hall, three rows of plastic-backed chairs were lined up along the side walls. The centre area remained open for dancing. Bride and groom proudly stood on stage beneath an apex of red and white crepe streamers. At the opposite end, a line of tables held selections of potluck supper. A huge punch bowl occupied the centre of its own table. Darrin's belly groaned in anticipation.

"There's Totah," Lisa said when she spied Grandpa sitting alone in a corner.

She took Naomi and began to carefully circulate. You didn't want to miss a single family member or friend. They might become offended. Mark and Brenda joined the tour while Darrin wandered about looking for Sharla. He felt uneasy at these gatherings. Adults always told you about when they changed your diaper and bounced you on their knee.

From the stage, a microphone whistled sharply. Band members plugged in amplifiers and twanged guitars. Darrin saw Fox unwrap his electric bass guitar. With Fox around, he realized he was safe from Arley.

Darrin got in line to eat. He heaped his paper plate with samples of everything. He didn't want to hurt anybody's feelings by not taking some of their speciality. He sat on a chair and chomped on a pickle. "Ahki!" He grimaced. Some dill pickle juices got on his sore lip and it stung so much it made his eyes' water.

He gulped his food down and patiently waited for Totah to finish eating. Weddings were a time of feasting so he went back to the table and stuffed his pockets with sweet pickles. They didn't hurt as much. He saw Totah tossing his plate in a big, metal garbage drum. He knew Totah could be trusted because he wasn't an adult. He was an elder.

"Se:kon Darrin," Totah said. He grabbed Darrin's hand and pumped it with enthusiasm. "By guh, you musta grow'd two inches since I last saw you." He smiled and two spaces in the bottom row of his tobacco stained teeth showed.

"Well...not exactly..."

"Ha-ha-ha! Not exactly he says." Totah rubbed his hooked nose with a bony knuckle. "Not exactly."

"Want a pickle, Totah?"

"Sure." He took one, wiped off some pocket fuzz and crunched on it. "It won't go too good with that punch I got there." He pointed to a paper cup sitting on a chair. "So maybe I just better have one."

"Are you gonna dance tonight, Totah?"

"Sure am." Totah sat down next to the cup. "I never missed one yet. Not even after my stoke."

"I want to tell you about a discovery I've made," Darrin said in a whisper.

"Uh-huh." Totah leaned forward. "A discovery?"

Darrin cupped his hand and held it to Totah's ear. "I know things," he whispered.

Totah looked puzzled. He smiled, thrust his chin forward and pulled on his billy goat beard. "What kind of things?"

"Stuff like how I knew Naomi was going to get born before anybody else knew it."

"Ah yes, I heard about that." Totah smiled in recognition. "It caused me to wonder."

"There's been other stuff too." Darrin pulled out a pickle and sat down. "Once, I made it lightning."

Totah paid full attention. "You made lightening come?"

"Yeah." Darrin happily crunched on his pickle. "I was mad at a bull, why?"

"Can you make other things happen?"

"No. But sometimes I know when things are going to happen."

"Whadda you mean?"

"Like today. I knew I was going to hit a home run and win the game."

"How'd you know that?"

Darrin pulled out his rabbit's foot. "Because *he* tells me." He handed the rabbit's foot to Totah. "When something's gonna happen he gets kinda warm."

Totah felt the rabbit's foot and dangled it. "It don't feel warm to me," he said.

"It's not warm now because nothing's gonna happen now."

Totah gave Darrin the rabbit's foot. "I used to know a seer once," he said. "Long time ago." He picked up his cup and took a drink. "Maybe you should go down to the river and see Truman Cloud. He's in atohwitshera and knows about orenda. He squashed his cup and flipped it into the metal garbage can. "Maybe he could help you."

From the corner of his eye, Darrin saw Sharla. "Well, uh, nyawen Totah." He stuffed the rabbit's foot into his pocket and pulled out a pickle. "Have another one. I, uh, I gotta go now."

"I'm full up," Totah smiled a knowing smile. "I guess when you gotta go you gotta go," he said. "Ha-ha-ha."

Darrin stuffed the pickle into his pocket and squeezed between bodies. He saw Sharla talking to an old woman standing by the stage. She smiled at him but quickly turned away. He caught his step, walked past them and headed out the side door.

To the west, storm clouds crowded the sunset and turned the air heavy. Darrin dodged between parked cars and slumped over the racetrack rail.

He sighed and looked at the ball diamond. I guess I shouldn't have pointed my bat over Arley's head, he thought. That's the *real* reason why I got beat up. For showing off! Boy, this seer stuff can really cause trouble. He heard gravel crunching behind him.

"I didn't know if you'd be here," said Sharla. "I don't think people should fight at wedding dances, do you? How are you feeling? Arley's here but you're not going to fight with him again are you?" She stood beside him and placed her elbows atop the rail.

From this angle, her long hair covered her face. Country music burst from the hall and three war whoops fractured the air in rhythm with the pounding of feet.

"I been here for a while," Darrin said, surprised at her sudden chatter. "I'll probably be okay in about a week."

She pushed at a stone with the toe of her sneakers and looked toward the sunset. Darrin felt a need to tell her about his visions. He shifted his weight from his right foot. What if she thinks I'm crazy, he thought.

Gusts of wind pushed a newspaper to mystically dance across the racetrack in front of them. "It's going to rain," Sharla predicted. "Yokennoron."

"Yoronhyoron tahnon tetyokarahs. It's going to thunder too," Darrin said.

Ric-rak-roounnn. A thunderclap drowned out the music from the hall.

"We'd better get back inside or we'll get soaked," Darrin said as big drops of rain splatted against the car roofs. "Yokennoron yah tewenhniseriyo."

Sharla smiled. "Let's just stay out here and get soaked," she said. "I love the fresh smell of rain."

Inky clouds spread through the darkening sky and Darrin saw a wall of rain approaching. "Come on," he tugged Sharla's arm. "We've got to get out of here. Hanyon oksa!"

Sharla pulled away and leaned against a car. "Go ahead, fraidy-cat." She flashed a defiant look.

Drops of rain peppered them and they stood as if frozen. They were testing each other to see who would run first. *Splat-splat-spat.* Darrin watched droplets turn Sharla's face shiny. Suddenly, she opened a car door and jumped inside. *Slam!*

He ran to the door but she pushed the button down and locked it. "Let me in," he pleaded.

Instead, she pulled hair from her brown eyes and shook her head. A giant flash illuminated the whole fairgrounds. *Rik-rac-karoommm!* The ground shook. Sharla threw open the car door. "Get in," she said.

Darrin heard rain pelting the roof of the car. He wondered if there would be any hailstones. He pulled up his T-shirt and patted his face. "I been in this car before. Is this your Dad's car?"

"Course it is, silly. I wouldn't just jump into anybody's car," she giggled. "It sure came in handy."

Wind howled and the car rocked. An explosion of light burst inside like a giant flashbulb transforming them into ghosts.

Sharla screamed. She fell against Darrin and put her head on his chest. "I'm scared." She covered her eyes with shaking fingers.

"I've got some pickles," Darrin said. He felt her body tighten and tremble with each thunderclap and lightning flash. It occurred to him that she didn't know about the Thunderers. Or West wind. "Don't worry. Our Grandfathers the Thunderers and his friends won't hurt you."

"Huh?"

"Totah says that our Grandfathers the Thunderers and their brother West Wind have always been good to the Onkwehonwe. It's North wind that you gotta watch out for."

"Do you believe in that Old Indian stuff?"

"I know that Totah never lies."

She raised her head and a quizzical look raced across her face. "You know your heart's got a crazy beat to it? She giggled. "Sometimes it even skips a couple of beats."

"Really?"

"It goes bomp-bomp-bomp, ba-ba bomp..."

"Yeah, right."

"...and then ba-ba, ba-ba, bomp."

"Next I suppose you're going to say it stopped."

"She pushed her lips into a sorrowful look. "Awww...I wouldn't want it to stop."

Darrin looked out the window. "It has stopped," he said. "Let's race to the hall."

"Darrin?" Sharla stretched toward him. "I think I've got something in my eye." She moved closer. "Can you see it?"

Darrin looked into her eye and Sharla gently kissed him. He looked at her in surprise. She threw her arms around him and kissed him again. "Oww!"

"Oh." Sharla covered her mouth. "I forgot about your sore lip...sorry if I hurt you."

"It's uh, nothing."

Darrin heard the *splash-splash-splash* of feet approaching. Before he could regain his composure the door opened and the interior lights went on.

A round face poked through the dim light. "What are you kids doin' in here?"

"Daddy?"

"Oh, um, we got stuck in here on account of the storm."

Sharla bounced across the seat and burst outside. "It's stopped." She ran toward the hall.

"You sure have a nice car." Darrin slid outside and ran after Sharla.

He wondered why adults made such a big deal about kissing themselves on TV all the time. He didn't think it was so hot. He caught up to Sharla and they ran up the steps and into the hall. Sharla giggled and disappeared into the crowd.

Darrin watched Fox skilfully playing his bass guitar. He had purple bulges over his eyes from his fighting days. From beneath a beaded vest, his arm muscles bulged out. He even sang some of the songs. Darrin wanted to start his lessons tonight. He wished the dance would hurry up and end.

"There you are," Brenda said. "I've been looking all over for you. Come on, we're going home now."

"What? How's come?"

"Because Totah's leaving and we're going with him."

"That's okay. I'll go home with Mark and Lisa."

"Mark and Lisa had a fight and they left."

"They had a fight?" Darrin felt his eyes bulge. "A real fight?"

"An argument, now let's go." Brenda pulled him by the ear.

"Ow! But I gotta see Fox."

"You can see Fox in the morning, now let's go."

During a bumpy ride home in Totah's battered car Darrin sulked. Instead of having his boxing lesson, he didn't even know if Fox would teach him. After they arrived, he flung the door open, bolted upstairs, threw off his clothes and climbed into bed.

He got hungry for sweet pickle. He pulled his pants up by a pant leg and took the last one from his pocket. He savoured it for a while on the good side of his mouth. He remembered Sharla's ravelled hair and her anxious face. He remembered the way the rain dripped off her shiny nose.

He chewed, swallowed and hoped his lip wouldn't be sore next time.

tsyata (7)

A Ride To The River

Darrin gathered up his clothes, put them on and plunged down the stairwell. If he caught the bare stud that framed the doorway at the bottom, he could swing out into the kitchen. Just like a trapeze guy in the circus.

He missed. Now out of control, he felt himself hurtling toward the iron stove. Twisting his body like a cat, he swerved and fell headfirst into the wood box.

"Morning Darrin," Brenda said. "What are you looking for?"

Darrin climbed out of the wood box. "I, uh, I've got business to do." He looked out the window and saw Fox in the potato patch. He started for the door.

"No you don't!" Brenda handed him a dish and spoon. "There's mush on the stove there...and brush your teeth when you're finished."

He gulped down his mush and tossed the utensils in the big pot on the stove. He brushed his teeth and threw the water outside. He filled the wash pan with clean water, threw in a towel and bar of soap and went outside. He put the pan on a stump and washed his face. "Ah'tso," he splashed water on his face. "It's cold this morning."

He planned not to let Brenda see him when he returned everything to the house. Adults couldn't rest until they found something for you to do. He thought: Wouldn't it be great if I could turn myself invisible?

From outside the house, Darrin stretched his arm inside. He had put everything in the pan and secretly pushed it to the centre of the wooden chair by the door. Success! Brenda hadn't seen him. He slunk into a mountain lion crouch and tip-toed along the wall of the house.

"Darrin!" Brenda's head shot from the doorway. "Where do you think you're going?"

"Oh, um, I've gotta see Fox about something. Right away."

"Well right-away git upstairs and put clean clothes on. And don't forget your underwear."

"Socks too?"

"Everything. Put 'em all in the hamper. I'm going to the Laundromat today so put all your dirty things in there."

Darrin sulked as he went back inside and trudged up the stairs to his room. One of these days I'm going to put something over on *her,* he thought. Yet deep down he knew everything she told him was right. One of these days I'll know everything too. But let her slip up just once, he promised himself. I'll get a bullfrog from the ditch and put in her bed. Gotcha!

After completing Brenda's instructions Darrin went outside. He noticed that half of the potatoes were all ready hilled.

"Heyyy-Fox," he said with gusto. "Working hard?"

Fox dropped his hoe and rushed toward him. He got behind Darrin and locked his arms around his chest. "Morning Darrin," he said.

Darrin felt himself being spun around. Air squeezed from his lungs. "I...need...your...help." Darrin gasped.

"What kind of help?"

Fox let go and Darrin fell to the ground. He had no neck; his head sat on his body like a pumpkin on a fence post. The lumps over his eyes were the same colour as the tattoos on his biceps.

Darrin got up. "I want you to teach me how to box."

At the word box, Fox crouched into a stance and raised his fists. In this position he seemed all arms and elbows. He transformed into a robot poised for action.

"You mean like this?" His smile dimmed into a killer-look. He feinted a punch toward Darrin. "Well come on, then. Put 'em up."

Darrin clenched his fists, walked toward Fox and

swung at his jaw. He felt a sting zap his belly as Fox stepped aside. "I want you to teach me." Darrin swung and missed. He felt another sting coming from his ear. It felt hot and started ringing. "Ow!" He put his hands down.

"Okay," Fox said. "I teach you how to box and you help me to take the horses for a bath...deal?"

"Deal."

"But I must inform you that these two hands are lethal weapons."

"Lethal weapons? Like the movie?"

"I dunno. That's what they told me when I got out of the army." Fox tossed the hoe to Darrin. "They said I can't use my hands to beat up any civilians because they're lethal weapons."

"I seen a movie called Lethal Weapon III." Darrin started to hoe. "But it wasn't about boxing."

"Funny thing about the army." Fox lit up a cigarette. "They teach you how to kill people but they won't let you beat anybody up. That never made any sense to me." He exhaled as he laughed. Smoke came out between his "ha-ha-ha's."

Fox let Darrin hoe while he finished smoking the cigarette. "Let's go then." He flicked the butt into the air. "You'll get your first lesson up at the barn. Bring the hoe."

Darrin put the hoe over his shoulder. During the

walk to the barn he started worrying about his aching face. He figured Fox would probably start by slapping him around. "My face is kinda sore," he said. "Some kid beat me up."

"Ah-ha!" Fox put up his dukes and began shadow boxing. "So that's why you want me to teach you."

"Well, I don't want to know everything like you. I just want to know enough to beat up a kid."

When they got to the barn Fox walked toward a pile of stones. "You're lucky Totah's gonna pour some concrete," he said taking the hoe from Darrin. "Otherwise, you'd have to find your own stones."

"Stones? What do we need stones for?"

"Go over there and stand next to the barn."

Darrin went over and stood beside the wall. He saw Fox pick up three of the stones. At first, he started tossing them up and catching them. Then he wound up and viciously threw one at Darrin's leg.

"Ow! What are you doing?" Another stone hit Darrin in the side. "Owww. That hurt!"

Fox laughed and threw another one. "Dodge them, then. Don't just stand there." He reached down and picked up three more stones. "That's lesson number one." He fired at Darrin's belly. "Footwork. You gotta be fast on your feet."

Darrin learned very fast. He stood and dodged and was soon able to make Fox miss. When Fox realized he couldn't hit him with stones anymore; he picked up the hoe and moved closer. He jabbed at Darrin with the handle and Darrin dodged. He kept lunging and jabbing. Darrin kept dodging until Fox was gasping for breath.

"Good work," Fox panted. He wiped off his brow. "Whew. Look at me sweat."

"Okay, when do we do punching?"

Fox reached into his pocket for a cigarette. "Damn," he said. "My matches are all wet. You got any matches?"

"Nah."

"Well, that's all for today." He replaced his cigarettes. "Let's take the horses to the river and go for a swim."

Darrin felt his face burning. He didn't like riding the horses because they didn't go where he wanted. They went where *they* wanted. Disappointment swept over him, he hadn't learned a single punch. At least his face would get refreshed in the cool water.

Fox opened the barn door. "Se:kon Clyde, se:kon Bonnie," he said. He walked toward their stall.

Clyde pawed the ground and blinked a big, glassy eye. His chestnut colour contrasted against his twitching black tail. He fluttered his lips as if answering. Bonnie turned her head. She was brown and had a white splotch on her face resembling the letter "B."

"Watch out for Bonnie," Fox said. "She's been biting

people lately." He threw a rope halter on the horses, adjusted it, and led them out of the barn. "You take Clyde. Here, let me help you up." He cupped his hand into a stirrup and bent down.

Darrin put his foot in Fox's stirrup and suddenly felt himself being flung over Clyde's back. He landed in the rose bush next to the barn doors.

"OOPS!" Fox reached down with his free hand while holding the halter ropes with the other. "You're gonna hafta put on some weight, boy. You're light as a feather."

Fox hoisted Darrin like a hydraulic lift. This time, he landed dead centre upon Clyde's broad, back. He held the rope rein with both hands and settled into Clyde's lopping stride. They clopped out the lane, went over a knoll and down the road.

Darrin grew uneasy. He knew that when they got out of Brenda's sight Fox would kick Bonnie into a gallop and Clyde would follow. He grabbed a handful of Clyde's thick, black mane. He wound it around the rope and clamped his hand tight as he could.

Clop-clop-clop.

Suddenly, Bonnie reared up and Fox flapped his arms to keep from falling off. Clyde jerked his head and Darrin saw a rabbit dart in front of them.

Eeeeheh-heh-heh-heh!

Bonnie leapt into full gallop. Clyde twisted his neck

and his eyes turned white. Darrin grabbed the rope with his other hand. Clyde lurched forward and exploded like a racehorse from a starting gate.

Hair blew into his eyes and Clyde's coarse mane slapped against his face. He blinked and squinted but all he could see were blurry images of trees, houses and barns. Up-down, up-down, up-down; the rope burned his hands. He yelled: "Are you okay, Fox?" He hoped yelling would somehow bring courage.

"Hang-on Darrin!"

Darrin let go of the rope and tried to wrap his arms around Clyde's neck. But they were too short, he couldn't lock his fingers together. He felt his legs start to slip from Clyde's sweaty back.

"I'm falling off!" He looked up toward Fox in desperation. He imagined that Fox would somehow save him.

"Hang in there." Fox looked back. "We're almost to the river. When we get there, do exactly what I do."

They stampeded over a hill. Darrin saw the river bouncing up and down like a flip-flopping TV screen. With every gallop, he felt himself slip a little more. Suddenly his body slid over the side but a sneaker hooked into Clyde's backbone groove.

Up-down, up-down, up-down.

As they plunged over the river bank, Darrin saw Fox crouch on Bonnie's back. When they hit the water, Fox flexed his legs and sprung-off. *Ka-splash.* Darrin fell off just as Clyde hit the water. The cool water splashed against his hot face and felt good.

"Ha-ha-ha." Fox stood hip deep in the water. "Good thing you fell off," he said. "Sometimes, those buggers will roll over on you."

Darrin saw an old man fishing. He sat peacefully on a log atop the river bank. His white hair had black steaks in it like marble. His skin was mahogany-coloured and he had a round face. Darrin expected him to say something about the disruption they caused. Yet he sat still as a turtle and watched them with piercing eyes.

Darrin waved at him and looked at Fox. "I hope that ole guy's not gonna be mad at us for scaring the fish away."

"Nah. That's old Truman Cloud. He won't get mad. He's a man of peace."

"Yeah, but look at him. Just the way he sits is kinda...kinda powerful."

"Ha-ha-ha." Fox flexed his biceps. "Power? Now this is power. He rubbed his fist against Darrin's nose."

"Does he catch lots of fish?"

"I dunno. They say he knows nikahneka'a. They say Atohwi has the orenda to cure people." Fox reached into his pocket. "Otah! My cigarettes are all wet."

"So he knows how to cure people, eh?"

"Yeah. He knows all that Indian stuff. He goes to Onondaga Longhouse."

"Where does he live?"

"Over there." Fox cupped his hand. "See that little log house in the willows." He skimmed a handful of water at Darrin's face. "Come on," he said. "Race you to the other side."

"What about the horses?"

"Don't worry. They'll stay in the water and drink."

They peeled off everything except their underpants and threw their clothes on the bank. A thick branch used as a diving board overhung the river on the other side. Darrin churned water like a paddle wheel boat and got there first. He pulled himself up, ran out on the branch and cannonballed Fox. *Ka-splash!*

"I guess we know who the champion swimmer is," he said while dog-paddling furiously.

Fox gasped for air. "Now you know why you shouldn't smoke cigarettes." He spat out a stream of water.

Darrin wondered why adults always lectured you on how to be healthy. Then they turned right around and did something unhealthy. Like smoking. He remembered the coloured pictures of a smoker's lung he saw in school once. It looked like a brain that had turned brown. It had bloody scabs all over it. Yecchhh! Maybe adults aren't so smart after all.

They swam back across the river. They threw water on the horses, wiped them down and lay on the bank to rest. Darrin saw the old man carrying his tackle box back to his cabin.

"Let's go visit Truman Cloud," Darrin said.

Fox swept his palm across his forehead. "I wouldn't."

"Why not? You scared or something?"

"Lookit. I know how to fight, right? And my hands are lethal weapons." Fox put his dukes up in front of his chest. "And I can lick anybody on the reserve. But there's some things you just leave be. Same reason an alligator don't mess with a turtle. Understand?"

"Got it."

"Hey, we gotta get back, it's past lunch time."

They put on their jeans, slung their shirts over their shoulders and stuffed socks into their pockets. They slipped into their sneakers, climbed on top of the horses and clopped home. Fox pointed to the gravel road that paralleled the river. "Where do you think that road goes?" he asked.

"Ohsweken. You *know* it goes to the village."

"Nah." Fox grinned. "It don't go nowhere's. Ha-ha-ha!"

Darrin relaxed. He knew the horses wouldn't run anymore. Even if their tails were on fire. So far, today was a good day. He had survived his footwork lesson and the stampede in one piece.

He craned his neck toward the little log house. Totah confided to him that the Atohwi had cured his stroke. He concluded that some things had powers above ordinary men. So that's where Truman Cloud lives, he thought. He looked at Fox's bulging muscles. I wonder what kind of power is going to help me?

tsatekon (8)

The Elephant Dream

Two slits of hatred glared at Darrin beneath purple scar tissue. This was the first time they were sparring. Fox seemed transformed into a grizzled stranger, a wolverine, a killer-creature.

For the past two weeks, Darrin gained little punching experience. True, he learned the difference between a jab, a cross, a hook, an uppercut and a bolo punch. He knew combinations and Fox showed him how to set them up. He could throw a haymaker all the way from his toes and keep his balance. But mostly it was footwork, footwork, footwork.

It wasn't enough to throw stones and jab at him. Fox made him jump rope. Just like a girl. This regimen had made him quick. Fox couldn't even hit him any more. He could float like a butterfly.

He noted that boxing training had improved his baseball playing. The season had started but Sharla hadn't come to see any games. He wondered why.

When he won the position as right fielder, Arley quit the team. He said baseball was a sissy's game and he'd rather play lacrosse. Darrin found out the true reason; Arley was too old and thus ineligible.

Yet even though his feet were quick, he didn't feel up to fighting Arley. He needed more help with his punching. He needed quick hands as well as quick feet. He needed to sting like a bee.

Fox stuck out his chin. "Go ahead, hit me," he said. "*If* you can."

Darrin clenched his fists. He crouched into a fighter's stance and jabbed at Fox's chin. He missed. He jabbed and missed again.

"Come on, boy. Kill! Kill! Put something into it!"

Darrin started dancing counter clockwise. Every time he missed Fox, he got a little madder. He couldn't seem to land a single punch. It was like fighting a ghost.

"Just remember this," Fox said. "You pick the time and place when you fight somebody." He did a double-pump shuffle with his feet. "That way, you take 'em by surprise, eh?"

Thok-thok!

Darrin felt two stings from his forehead. He put his hands up in front of his face.

"Don't *do* that," Fox punched Darrin's belly. "How are you gonna see these punches comin' at you?"

Darrin pulled his hands down so he could see. *Thok!* He took one the ribs and grimaced. He threw a right but Fox blocked it with his forearm.

"Come on, Darrin," Fox frowned in disgust. "Use your speed. What have I been teaching you?"

Suddenly, Darrin's mind began transposing Fox into a new picture. His eyes got blurry; he couldn't quite make things out. His ears heard a sound like a waterfall. *ARRRRRrrrrr.*

He seemed to be moving to and fro. Something was coating his face and he touched a finger to his cheek. Moisture. His eyes cleared and he felt his jaw drop in awe.

He was riding on the back of a black elephant! Its gentle rolling gait seemed like a porch swing but there was white water beneath them. He turned around and saw two other black elephants sloshing along behind. They seemed to be struggling against a rushing current. They were trying to stop being pushed toward the edge of Niagara Falls!

Suddenly, Darrin's elephant slipped. It struggled for balance on mossy rocks but it didn't fall down. Darrin heard the other two elephants cry out in unison. *Eeeeeeaaaa!* One of them fell. The raging current pushed its bulky body past them. It slid along, hopelessly trying to stand up. Instead, it slowly went around and around. It spun into deeper water.

Darrin realized he'd have to turn his elephant toward shore. With both hands, he yanked the elephant's right ear. He jumped up and down digging his feet into its back. The soft heels of his sneakers had little effect. They couldn't penetrate the elephant skin. He tried pounding his fist on the elephant's lumpy head but it was no use. They were loosing their battle to the current.

Through the thick mist, Darrin saw the edge of the falls. It was only ten feet away! The first elephant reached the brink. At the last second it tried to turn but went over sideways. *Eeeeeeaaa!*

Darrin felt his elephant stumble to its knees. It rocked and even used its trunk to regain a footing. Darrin tried to yell for help. "Herrmmff! Herrmmff!" he hollered.

The second elephant passed them and disappeared over the edge of the falls. Darrin's elephant swerved and almost knocked him off. They had turned completely around and now faced up river. He felt his elephant's back slump. He saw its stubby back feet dangling over the brink.

Darrin climbed to the elephant's forehead. He felt it start to slip. A jagged rock lay an inch beneath the rushing water. He gathered all his strength and leapt from the elephant just as it went over. *Eeeeeeaaa!* His finger tips caught the rock but they slipped on the slimy moss. He clawed with his finger nails but they still slipped off.

Oh no, he thought. Nooooooo. His belly felt queasy, like when you go over a roller-coaster hill. Nooooo.

Thok!

Darrin felt his head snap back. He saw another one of Fox's fists coming but it was too late. *Thok!* He decided to pay strict attention; Fox meant business.

"Come on, man." Fox snorted. "Get with it. Kill, kill!"

Darrin saw a punch coming toward his belly. He side stepped it. Fox tried a combination but Darrin avoided it. Darrin bobbed and a right-cross whizzed past his nose. A left jab almost caught him but he warded it off with his forearm.

"Come, on man, hit me." Darrin glared at Fox. "What's the matter? Too many cigarettes?" He dropped his hands and danced dangerously close to him.

Fox dropped his hands and spread out his arms. He leapt at Darrin and tackled him. On the way down, Darrin rabbit punched him. Fox began tickling his belly. Darrin tried to punch his face but Fox grabbed his arms and pinned him.

"That's more like it," Fox said. "Now you're catching on. You can't get beat up if nobody can hit you."

"Well, I didn't hit *you*, either."

"But you would have if I didn't flop you," Fox gasped for air.

"When I am going to be able to flop you?"

Fox lifted Darrin to his feet. He lit a cigarette, exhaled and placed his arm on Darrin's shoulder. They headed toward the house.

"You'll *never* be able to flop me," Fox laughed. "Not for a while anyway. I leave for my new ironworker job in New York tomorrow. I'll be up in the sky walking the beams with the birds."

Darrin shook-off Fox's arm. "Really? You can't go to work now. You haven't taught me enough, I'm still a lousy puncher."

"You're fine. You don't need any more lessons, just keep workin' on your footwork. You can always use the hay bales in the barn for punching bags, you know."

Darrin shrugged. "I guess it doesn't matter much anyway. I just don't have a killer instinct like you."

"Don't worry about that, everybody's got one. You get mad enough and it'll come." Fox smiled. "And when it does, you'll just feel like bustin' somebody's head. Ha-ha-ha!"

Darrin kicked at the ground. "I hope you're right, Fox. I sure hope you're right."

It occurred to Darrin that he should share his vision about the elephants with Fox. After all, they were fighting buddies now and friends always shared their dreams. Fox was cool, he'd understand.

"Fox, did you see any elephants lately?"

"Elephants? What kind of elephants?"

"You know, the kind in the zoo."

"I dunno." Fox took another drag. "I never been to a zoo."

"Well anyway, I just saw three of them while we were fighting."

Fox looked at him and smiled. "Them weren't elephants, dummy," he said. "They were my fists punching you in the eye. Ha-ha-ha." Fox put his knuckles against Darrin's head and rubbed. "Noogies," he said. He bolted toward the house. "Race you to dinner."

"Ahki!" Darrin massaged his burning, scraped head. He didn't feel like running anywhere. His eyes dropped as he trudged toward the house.

Darn you Fox, he thought. I don't care what you said about leaving things alone. I'm going to get rid of these silly vision-things once and for all. I'm going to visit Truman Cloud tomorrow. If he can get rid of heart sickness, he'll know how to get rid of vision sickness too.

He skipped up the steps and went into the house to eat his supper.

tyohton (9)

The Visit

Next morning, Darrin finished his chores. He remembered that neither Bonnie nor Clyde was reliable. Riding one of them to the river would be risky so he took his bike. It made no sense to leave anything to chance in case he had to escape from Truman Cloud.

He could control his bike, even though it was rickety and had plenty of squeaks and moans. Dust caked its sprockets and its wheel cones were loose. It rolled freely, but its thin tires wobbled. Darrin sped out the lane pumping his legs like pistons. He didn't want Brenda to interrupt this important journey.

He threw the back wheel into a skid as he turned onto the dusty, gravelled road. He clamped his hands to the handlebars, stood up and pumped like a sprint runner. He sped past the corner out of Brenda's voice range.

His thoughts turned to Truman Cloud. He didn't know how to behave in the presence of a medicine man. True, he had attended spiritual ceremonies at Sour Springs Longhouse with Totah. He knew many elders still practised and taught the secrets of the universe. But Truman belonged to a different Longhouse. What if he practised bad medicine?

He pumped along the road listening to the chain rubbing against the frame. He let go of the handlebars and coasted down the road. A stone kicked up and strummed his spokes. *Brunnng.* He rode over the last hill and saw the river. He held the handlebar with one hand and pretended to hold a microphone in the other.

He said, "Flight two-niner to tower; two-niner to tower. Request landing instructions, over."

Wind blew hair from his eyes as the bike picked up speed. He squeezed both handgrips to apply the brakes but nothing happened. There were no brakes!

He yelled: "Pilot to crew, pilot to crew. Bail out! Bail out!" He tried to stop by twisting the bike sideways into a skid. It didn't work. He zoomed straight into the ditch.

He felt himself being catapulted through the air. He went one way, the bike the other. He tumbled to a stop and saw the bike plummet into the river. *Splash!*

He noticed blood on his elbow and wiped it off with

a hollyhock leaf. He got mud on his sneakers when he pulled the bike from the water. He pushed it up the bank toward Truman's log cabin.

He leaned the bike against a thick tree. It had a hole big as a concrete block cut from it. Darrin positioned the bike so it faced the road. He wanted it ready in case he needed to escape. Maybe Fox was right about leaving Truman alone.

Looking at the house, he saw one of the curtains move! He jumped behind the tree and took a deep breath to hold his stomach in. A shiver ran up his spine as he checked for further movement. He heard a rustling sound. *Caw! Caw! Caw!* Wings flapped. He looked at the window but a reflection from the sun blinded him.

"Hey, you!" Truman held a knife in one hand and leaned upon his cane with the other. "What are you doin' there?"

"I, uh. I came to visit you. My Totah said I should see you about something."

"You ride your bike poorly," Truman said. "Well, come on then. I'm doing some carving now so you'll have to come inside." He disappeared around the corner.

Darrin reluctantly walked toward the cabin, curiosity pushing him forward. Turning its corner, he saw a snapping turtle hanging from a tree. It had a wire around its neck and blood dripped from a cut in its tail. He felt something flutter in his belly.

"Sataweyat," Truman motioned with the knife. He sat down on a chair, picked up a wooden block and started carving.

Darrin stepped inside and took off his sneakers. In the centre of the kitchen, a picnic table stood with two chairs around it. Three bass-heads lay on a blood-spattered newspaper beside a porcelain pan. Six black, fish-eyes stared at him.

"Satyen enitskwara'tsherake," Truman said. "Oh nahoten yesayats?"

Darrin sat down. "Darrin ne yonkyats," he said softly.

"Tsi'tenha kiken," Truman held up his carving. "Waton tweet, tweet." He laughed. "Sanahskwayen ken nise tsi' tenha?"

"Toka," Darrin said. He knew Truman said something about birds. He wished he had paid more attention to his language lessons in school. "Toka."

"Ha, ha, ha," Truman smiled. "You don't know if you have a bird? Maybe you are a bird?"

Darrin meditated on Truman's words. Adults always knew stuff kids didn't understand but what do birds have to do with it?

"Oh, that's all right," Truman said. "We can talk in tyohrhenhsa, English language, then."

Darrin saw a red, contorted face mask hanging on the wall with its eyes covered. He recognized that the hair on its head was really horse hair. It cascaded over both ears and almost reached the floor. He wondered why a rag covered its eyes. But you didn't ask questions of your host, especially when he's a medicine man. If he wanted you to know something he'd tell you.

"I came to see you because I need a doctor," Darrin blurted it out. "And Totah said you can cure sickness."

"Sanonhwaktani ken?" Truman looked concerned. "Are you sick?"

"Well, sort of."

"Is it physical or is it in your head?" Truman carefully studied Darrin's brown eyes.

"I'm all right but sometimes, I um, I feel things are going to happen and they really happen."

Truman put his knife on the table and wrapped the fish heads with the newspaper. "Satonhkaryaks ken?" He set the bundle on a shelf and waited for Darrin's answer.

Darrin remembered a Brenda lecture about not taking food from strangers. If even if you're hungry. But Truman wasn't a stranger, he was a medicine man. You can't offend somebody in their own house by not accepting hospitality.

"Wakenya tathens," he said. "I'm thirsty."

Darrin watched Truman go the refrigerator and reach inside. He glanced around the room and saw glass jars neatly stacked on shelves. Some contained roots while some enclosed different coloured leaves. Some had dried cherry pits and others had coloured kernels of Indian corn.

He saw horse tails hanging on the walls and braided, weed-like things. To understand them, they needed handling and they needed smelling. He knew you didn't fondle objects that didn't belong to you. If elders wanted you to touch something they'd hand it to you. Truman handed him an old, metal cup with U.S. Army etched into the handle.

"Oh nahoten kiken?" Darrin asked. "What is this?"

"Ohnekawisto," Truman smiled. "Cold water."

Darrin took a drink. "Yohnekano," he said, "the water is cold." He looked into Truman's clear eyes. "I worry that if I tell people what's going to happen, I'll get laughed at."

"How do you know when something's going to happen?"

Darrin reached into his pocket. "This here rabbit's foot starts to get hot." He held it up. "Do you think it has some kind of magic?"

Truman put his cup down, took the rabbit's foot and stroked it. Then he put it between the palms of his hands. "When you see these things happen do you see them as yourself, or are you somebody or something else?"

"What do you mean?"

"Do you turn into something? Say, a bird?"

Darrin pondered. "No. I'm always myself."

"You should be careful to sing your song, he gave Darrin the rabbit's foot. "Others have shared your dilemma."

"They have? Who?"

"I will tell you about a little bird who learned to value his uniqueness." Truman pushed back his chair and crossed his arms. "Ta ne'kati, a long time ago, all the birds wanted to sing the sweetest song on Mother Earth. To learn it, they would have to visit the home of the Creator located in the highest sky.

"Kestrel, Hawk, Goose and Swan all tried hard as they could but none could make it. The ones with colourful feathers like Woodpecker, Cardinal, and Oriole couldn't fly high enough. Neither could Golden Pheasant or Wood Duck.

Truman took a drink of water. "One day, Eagle said he would try. He was Lord of the feathered ones and could fly the highest. Since all of the bird families had failed, they hoped Eagle would succeed.

"While preparing for his rigorous flight, Eagle spread his great wings. Everybody admired them except a little bird who sneaked out from under a pine tree. He hopped upon Eagle's back and quickly slipped beneath his feathers. Nobody saw him. He was brownish-grey like a Sparrow but a little bigger. He had a rusty tail.

"Ta ne'kati, Eagle flew higher and higher until he approached the clouds. The little bird had never flown so high before. They were above the clouds and went even higher but the home of the Creator was still higher." Truman waved his cup.

"Eagle became exhausted and he started to turn back. The little bird flew off his back and continued. He was rested and didn't need as much air to breathe as Eagle. Up, up, up he flew until he saw the bright light where sweet songs are sung from all sides.

"Ta ne'kati, he lit and listened to all the beautiful songs. He copied the sweetest one he heard and sung it over and over. When he knew every note, he flew back to Mother Earth." Truman put his cup down.

"During his long flight home, he became concerned that Eagle would be angry. He was afraid Eagle might even decide to kill him. The others would either be mad at him or be jealous of his best song." Truman looked at Darrin. "What do you think he should do?"

Darrin took a drink and pondered. If Eagle killed the little bird, nobody would ever hear the Creator's beautiful song. If all the other birds were mad at him or jealous, he couldn't change them. "I dunno," he said. He put his cup on the table.

"Ta ne'kati, he decided to take appropriate action. He knew that he had good camouflage and could scarcely be seen in the forest. He blended right in. So he found a thick grove with bushes all around. Here, he could do his duty and share his beautiful song. He could sing and feel proud that he was different from all the others." Truman solemnly looked at Darrin. "To this day, those are the places where the song of the Hermit Thrush is most often heard."

Truman's eyes shone like two crystal pools with a light behind them. He stood up, grabbed his cane and limped toward the doorway.

Normally, Darrin wouldn't question an elder. That was impolite. Yet something seemed to push him. After all, he came for an answer, not another question.

"Why didn't he share the song with Eagle?" he asked. He slipped into his sneakers and followed Truman to a wooden shed.

"Well, think on it a minute." Truman carried a hoe and shovel squeezed under an arm. He tossed an empty coffee can to Darrin. "Come on," he said. "Let's get some worms. Why don't you tell me?"

They walked along the riverbank until Truman found an area where plenty of worms lived. He dug and turned over a shovel of sod. "Put the fat ones in your can," he said. "Try as I might, I can't get them to jump in." He winked. "Ha-ha-ha!"

"The Hermit Thrush couldn't make it on his own, so he used his wits," Darrin put a worm into the coffee can. "He got the song that everybody wanted. He won, right?"

"Do you think the story is about winning and losing?"

Darrin put another worm in the can. "Well, he won, but he also lost."

Truman turned over another shovel of sod. "Why do you think he lost?"

"Well, he got the song, but he has to be careful when he sings it." Darrin put two more worms into the can.

After they caught enough worms, they returned their digging equipment to the shed and went fishing. On the river bank Truman handed Darrin an old fish line wrapped around a stick like a kite string. "Do you know how to fish with a line or do you use a pole?"

"I use a rod and reel that we keep in the barn."

"Well watch me, then." Truman squeezed a fat worm on his hook. He gave the fishing line a whirl and released it. The sinker carried it half-way across the river. *Splash!* "Do you think the Creator gave him the song and let him keep it so he wouldn't use it?"

Darrin gave his line a whirl. It splashed into the water right in front of them. He pulled it in and tried again. This time he managed to release it correctly.

"How's that," he beamed. It almost went out as far as Truman's line.

Truman caught two plump, bull-heads then they went back to his cabin. "I'm glad you came by today," he said.

Today? The word struck Darrin like a sharp pain. He said today! Have I been here the *whole* day? Oh no, now I've done it, Darrin thought. Brenda's gonna have a fit for sure. Here comes the ole Eagle-eye again.

"After we eat these fish, I'll show you how to make a turtle shell rattle. He should be all drained-out by now."

"Well I can't." Darrin jumped to his feet. "I gotta get home right now. Nobody knows where I went and I'm supposed to tell Brenda where I'm going."

"Okay, maybe next time. Be more careful on your bike. Onekiwahi, Darrin."

"Onekiwahi."

Darrin burst from the cabin and hopped upon his bike. The chain caught against the guard, locked the back wheel and flipped him off. He got up and kicked it free but it bent into a weird shape. He pushed the handlebars along and hopped upon the seat. His ankle got scrubbed when he stood up to pump the pedals. Darrin knew he had to be home before dark. Or else.

As he raced home he thought about the Hermit Thrush. Hermit Thrush bird is the opposite of what it seems. It's a little bird but it has the biggest song. I wonder if *opposite* applies to the dream I had. What could the opposite of three black elephants falling over a waterfall be? Could it be three white mice flying up into the air?

Anyway, Darrin didn't have time to worry about that now. He had to worry about Brenda.

oyeli *(10)*

Lisa and Naomi Come Home

He almost ran into a car at the corner and hurdled over the ditch to take a short cut. He pedalled across the field and crashed into the basswood tree to stop. He fell off the bike and limped into the house. Darn! Pain burned his ankle.

Brenda was lighting a kerosene lamp. "Well, I'm glad to see you," she said. She put it on the table next to a pizza box and walked toward him. "I wondered where you went," she whimpered. She gave Darrin a big hug.

Darrin pulled away to look into her eyes. Could she be crying? Yep, those were tears all right. She must have thought something happened to me. Probably thought I got killed or something. No sense lying at a time like this because when adults cry, everything is okay. You can get away with anything.

"I went to visit Truman Cloud," Darrin said. He heard a baby crying from upstairs.

She wiped her eyes with the corner of her apron. "Truman Cloud? Down-by-the-river Truman Cloud?"

"Yep. He's a pleasant ole guy. I helped him find some worms and we went fishing. I didn't catch anything though."

"Did you eat?"

Darrin was hoping she'd ask. "Truman offered to feed me," he smiled. "But I remembered your advice and didn't take anything."

"That's good because Lisa brought a pizza with her from town," Brenda sniffled. "Neither of us are very hungry right now. You can have the whole thing."

Darrin hopped on a chair and opened the box. "Who's pop is this?"

"You can have that too."

Lisa always bought Hawaiian-style pizza. It had big chunks of pineapple and was Darrin's favourite. He couldn't believe his good fortune. Listening to Brenda was starting to pay off. Still, he wondered why Lisa came here so late in the day. She had never visited them after supper before.

"I didn't see Mark's car," Darrin gulped. The pizza was cold.

Lisa emerged from the stairwell. "There, that ought to hold Naomi for a while. "Hi, Darrin," she sniffled. "How's my big brother?"

Darrin noticed that her eyes were red and puffy.

What's the matter with these guys, he thought. Did they both think I got killed? Why am I suddenly Lisa's *big* brother? Why aren't they eating any pizza?

"What's the matter with youse?" Darrin put down his slice and took a gulp of pop. "How many pieces should I save for Mark?"

Lisa walked over and hugged Darrin's head. "Mark's not here," she said. "You can have all of them."

Brenda reached over and took two slices from the box. "Here, let me warm these up for you." She put them on the stove.

That did it. Anytime adults treated you like this they were up to something. But what could it be?

Brenda brought over a big slice of warm pizza and took his old one back to the stove. "I'll warm this one up for you too," she said.

Lisa sat down and watched him eat. With all this attention, he decided not to ask any more questions. He couldn't talk with his mouth full anyway. He'd just observe everybody and eventually find out everything.

Lisa winked at him. A tear rolled down her cheek. In a shaky voice she said, "Mark and I have split up. Naomi and I are going to be living here at Totah's for a while."

Darrin chewed on his pizza. He swallowed and washed it down with a gulp of pop. He accidentally brushed his ankle against a table leg. "Ahki!" he said.

Lisa reached across the table, held his hand and patted it. "I knew you'd take this hard, but don't worry," she sniffled and forced a smile. "Everything will be all right."

"Aren't you going to live at the Lafont's anymore?"

"No."

Darrin pulled his hand away and took a bite of pizza. Darn, he thought. There goes my secret money supply. It's a long ride but I guess I can still go and visit good ole Mr. Lafont.

"Are the Lafont's moving?"

"No. Why do you ask?"

Darrin put down his pizza, raised up his leg and showed them his bruised ankle. "I got hurt coming home on my bike," he announced to his attentive audience. "I didn't want to be late and I got hurt." He massaged his ankle.

Brenda came over and started to message it for him. "Well, it's not going to stop you from dancing tomorrow, is it?" Brenda looked concerned.

"Dancing?"

"It's powwow time," Lisa said. "Did you forget?"

"Powwow time? Tomorrow?"

"That's right," Brenda said. "So you better git to bed soon as you finish eating."

So that's it, Darrin thought. That's why they've been so kind to me. I'll bet I have to sleep in the barn tonight. I'll bet Lisa and Naomi took over my room. "Where am I going to sleep?" he asked.

"You've got your choice," Brenda said. A lamp reflection in her glasses made her eyes flicker. "You can sleep with Lisa and Naomi or sleep in the barn."

No way did he want to sleep with Lisa and Naomi. "There's too many snakes in the barn," Darrin said, putting his foot down. "Ahki! I'll sleep on the car seat on the porch."

"You can sleep on the floor in the front room," Lisa said in her sweetest tone.

"Nah, it's warm tonight." Darrin took another bite of pizza and burped. "The porch'll be better." He tipped his pop too far and it stung his nose. "Ahki!"

In an instant, Brenda handed him an Army blanket and a pillow. "As soon as Fox leaves for New York you can have his room," she said.

"Cool," Darrin said. He tucked them under an arm, grabbed the last piece of pizza and went down the hallway to the front porch. He pushed his shoulder against the front door to open it.

"Lisa," he yelled. "I'm glad you're back home. You and Naomi can have my room for as long as you need it." He pushed the door closed.

He made up his bed and gazed at the stars. Crickets, frogs and fireflies were in abundance at this time of year. He figured Lisa would be better off in his room anyway. Mark worshipped money too much. Maybe that's why they split up. He heard a mosquito buzz.

He wondered if Sharla would come to the powwow tomorrow. He guessed she'd be there like everybody else on the Rez. The powwow was a good meeting place. Onkwehonwe came from great distances and brought their food and crafts to sell. Unlike serious religious ceremonies in the longhouse, powwows were more like social gatherings. You could even win money in the dance competitions. He felt mosquitos lighting on his arm.

He determined a strategy he'd use to get to know Sharla better. He brushed at the mosquitos. Instead of entering the competition dances, he'd dance Inter-tribal dances with her all day. Inter-tribals allowed competitive dancers a rest and let the audience participate.

He devoured the pizza, slipped beneath the scratchy army blanket, and listened until the crickets faded away...

enska yawenre (11)

The Powwow

Next morning when Darrin awakened, a new 'why' crowded his thoughts. If Truman was able to cure people from their illnesses, then why didn't he offer to help? Surely he knew how to drive away dreams. Especially bad dreams. Maybe these dreams weren't as bad as he thought.

After mush with Brenda, Lisa and Naomi, he bounded upstairs to his room. On powwow days he always seemed to be fixing his dancing clothes at the last minute. Today, Lisa would help Brenda do the chores and he'd have plenty of time.

He looked under the bed and couldn't believe his eyes. His ribbon-shirt, buckskin leggings, war club, beaded belt and moccasins were missing. So were his roach and breechcloth. He ran to the dresser and slid open the bottom drawer. Instead of his tobacco pouch, bear claw necklace and deer hoof anklets he found women's skirts. In place of his silver arm bands and beaded rosettes, he found women's sweaters.

He looked on top of the stud where he kept his beads and needles. His awl, wax-chunk and nylon thread were missing too. He tore open the big black chest. His kahstowa, feathered bustle and sleigh bell anklets weren't inside. Naomi's baby clothes replaced them.

"Lisa!" He ran down the stairwell, caught the stud and swung out twice before releasing it. "Where did you put all my onkwehonwe stuff?" He landed with a thud.

"It's out in the barn."

"Oh-no! The mice'll eat my leggings." He ran toward the door and threw it open. He heard Lisa start to giggle.

"I was only teasing," she laughed. "Just because I lived in the city doesn't mean I turned dumb. I put all your stuff in the front room."

Darrin turned and flashed a toothy grin at Lisa. He held it while he walked across the kitchen. When adults lie, it's teasing, he thought. When kids tell a lie you either get the ole Eagle eye or you get ignored. He went into the front room.

He found everything neatly packed in cardboard boxes. He admired Lisa's workmanship then dumped everything on the floor. He found his bead vials, arranged a work space and sat on the floor. He had to repair the beading on his belt.

"How come you made such a mess?" Brenda leaned against the doorway. "Lisa and I have decided to chip in and pay your entry fee at the powwow today. How much you need?"

Darrin saw Lisa peak from behind Brenda. "I'm not going to dance for money today," he said. "My ankle's too sore."

"You could at least get fourth," Lisa said. "I know it's not three hundred dollars but anything's better than nothing."

Brenda knelt down beside him and squeezed his shoulder. "How much does fourth pay?"

"I dunno. I never finished fourth, I always win."

"You always win?" Lisa smiled with delight.

Brenda nodded. "Yeah, he does," she smiled. He's even got money in the bank."

"But I'm not lending anybody anything," Darrin frowned. "Besides, this year I have to change my dance classification. I'd be dancing in Young Men's Traditional. Those guys are all a lot older than me."

"I think you could win," Lisa said.

"Not with my sore ankle. Not against the big guys."

Brenda got up and sighed. "Then you can work in the Recreation Committee's booth and help us out." She marched away. "We always need volunteers."

"Or, you can watch Naomi for me." Lisa picked out a green-fringed shawl from one of the boxes. "I've got a lot of dancing to catch up on." She put the shawl around her shoulders and twirled out the doorway.

Darrin finished beading his belt. He carefully inspected every feather to make sure none would fall off. At these western style powwows, they made a big deal out of it if you drop a feather on the ground. They stop everything and all the war veterans have to dance in an honouring ceremony. Then they make you claim your feather right in front of the whole audience.

He decided against taking his war club. It was too cumbersome to attach to his belt and would require holding. He wanted his hands free in case he got Sharla to sit beside the river with him. He packed everything in two paper bags and placed them in the trunk of Totah's Ford.

Powwows were fun and he wished Totah would come with them. He didn't attend these Plain's Indian spectacles because the dancing competition prizes were money. Instead, he preferred the old way. He drummed the Rotinonhsonni water drum and danced with Darrin at Longhouse socials. He told Darrin to always use the gifts that the Creator provided. Never forget your own dances and songs.

It didn't take long before they left. In Totah's absence, Brenda drove his old car with the big steering wheel. She didn't drive often and Lisa had to help her negotiate turns.

When they arrived at Chiefswood parking lot, Darrin decided to dance in Grand Entry. Anything was better than getting stuck watching Naomi. He usually changed clothes in the car but with two women and a baby around he went to the men's restroom.

Not being a contestant, he could wear his kahstowa. Feather position in an Rotinonhsonni kahstowa denoted tribe; Mohawks wore three eagle feathers pointing up. When competing, he usually wore a roach and his feathered bustle. Today he left them at home.

He dressed in a corner and put his rabbit's foot into a beaded pouch. His ankle was still tender so he tied his deer hoof anklets around his knees. He wriggled to settle his onkwehonwe clothes. He rolled his other clothes into a ball, shoved it into a paper bag and placed it on a shelf. He scurried to the assembly area.

Dancers of all sizes and shapes were milling about. All of them wore their finest dance clothes. He looked for a familiar face, but couldn't find any. He went past all the fluorescent-coloured feathered dancers to the naturally coloured ones. That is where the traditional dancers stood and waited.

"Squeee...Welcome to the thirteenth annual Ouse

River Powwow," the announcer said. "Okay dancers! Step lively and may the Great Spirit smile on all of you today!"

Immediately, Darrin heard the shrieking cry of the big drum. Singers began their haunting song. Six men began beating in unison from the centre arbour and the dancers picked up their rhythm. Spectators shaded their faces and practised aiming their cameras.

Colour guards carried a great Eagle staff lined with feathers. Canadian and American flag bearers started to advance into the dance circle. Onkwehonwe veterans dressed in navy blue uniforms and tams followed them. Darrin felt his heart pounding in unison with the drum.

"Okay Men's Traditional, Let's go!" the announcer cried. "Let's Powwow! Hoka! Hoka! Hoka!"

From behind him, Darrin heard bells jingle. He saw an explosion of fluorescent colours when the Men's Fancy Dancers formed their line. Their black and white numbers were the only flaw in their colourful appearance. Behind them, sparkles flashed from the jingles on the dresses of the Women's Jingle Dress dancers.

Darrin approached a group of dancers behind the veterans. As hosts, Rotinonhsonnis danced in front during Grand Entry. He craned his neck toward the women hoping for a glimpse of Sharla. Crowd noise gave way to the two-step pounding of the drum. Darrin got behind a dancer and stepped into the circle. The Men's Traditional dancers closed in behind him.

Most Rotinonshonni dances were faster. Depending on their purpose, they used varying water drum rhythms and songs. Darrin felt his heart become consumed with the steady pulsing of the big drum. He shook his head and the Eagle and Hawk feathers of his kahstowa twisted freely. His deer hoof anklets picked up the rhythm and automatically raised and lowered his legs. His whole body flowed as if mixing his spirit with the drum.

"And now ladies and gentlemen, the Men's Traditional Dancers have entered the circle. Notice the authenticity of their dance clothes. Some of these dancers have come from as far away as New Mexico."

Darrin heard the shrieking cry of the singers. He could feel his pulse quicken with each thump of the big drum. His anklets rattled as his moccasins touched Mother Earth on the down beat.

"Here comes the Men's Fancy Dancers," the announcer said. "Notice their dance steps...Men's fancy."

At this angle, Darrin could see the Men's Fancy dancers enter. He heard their shiny bells jingle when each dancer twisted his body. He saw an explosion of rainbow colours as they stepped high. Some twirled and fell into leg splits on the down beat of the drum.

The dancers had made one complete circle around the arbour and more came in. Darrin saw the last of the Girl's Fancy dancers enter. He looked toward the Young Women's Traditional dancers. He saw Sharla two dancers ahead of the Jingle Dress dancers. The long fringes on her white buckskin dress swayed with dignity as she wafted along in perfect step.

Her black braids were long and she carried an Eagle wing. He had never seen her in onkwehonwe clothes before and she looked enchanting. Everybody danced around the circle until the last dancer from the Tiny Tots entered. They all stopped in unison on the last drum beat.

They stood and listened to the Flag Song, Traditional Invocation, Introduction of Dignitaries and Welcome. When the drum began for an Inter-tribal dance, Darrin gauged his step to overtake Sharla. He didn't want to just run over to her. No sense appearing anxious.

He danced next to her and pretended surprise. "Oh, se:kon Sharla. How are you doin'?"

She moved with a cloud's smoothness, her step clean and sure. "I'm fine, Darrin," she smiled. "I'm a little nervous. There sure are a lot of people here."

"Oh, that's okay," Darrin said. "I'm a little nervous myself."

"Where's your number? Aren't you competing?"

"Ah, no, not today...I've hurt my ankle. It's all sore and everything." Darrin stopped dancing. "Do you want to see it?" He lifted his leg.

Sharla kept going. "I'm going to do a speciality dance right after Tiny Tots." She disappeared behind two dancers.

Darrin began dancing again. Boy did I ever screw that up, he thought. She'll probably never speak to me again. I better make sure I watch her dance exhibition.

"Hi Darrin."

Darrin saw Lisa dancing next to him. "Se:kon Lisa," he said.

"Is that girl in the white buckskins Sharla?"

"Uh, yeah. Why?"

"Is she your girlfriend?"

"No. She's not my girlfriend," Darrin said. Here they go again with their boyfriend-girlfriend stuff. "Did Mark come to the powwow?"

"No. I don't think he'll be coming to Indian doings anymore."

"Is he ever gonna come and see us again?"

"I don't know. Mark thinks he can own everything. Even people." Lisa adjusted her shawl. "He expected me to take that job at Cobe's just so we could move out of the elephant house and get a bigger..."

"Elephant house?" Darrin stopped dancing. "What do you mean *elephant* house?"

Lisa stopped dancing and looked at him. "Elephant house. That's what we called it because on the Lafont's mail box it says L. Lafont."

Darrin turned and started for the dressing room. "Onenkiwahi," Lisa. "I gotta go."

Darrin dodged between dancers and broke into a trot. That's it, he thought. That's gotta be it. Those three elephants in my dream represent the two Lafont's and me. In the story of the Hermit Thrush, the little bird is the opposite of what it seems. The opposite of water is fire. The Lafont's house is going to burn down!

He opened his pouch and took out his rabbit's foot. By the time he got to the entry gate he felt it starting to get warm. He put it back. He ducked under the rope fence that ringed the dance area. He dodged people sitting in folding chairs. He had to help the Lafont's before they burned up!

He jogged past the food and craft booths on the midway. He saw Sharla and pretended not to notice her.

"Darrin!" she yelled. "I'd like you to meet my Aunty Karen."

Darrin came to a halt. "Hello Aunty Karen."

Aunty Karen said, "Sharla's going to do her Speciality Dance in about ten minutes. You could sit next to me in her folding chair and watch."

"I, I can't. I've got to go somewhere's right now." He broke away and ran up the hill.

As he approached the restrooms, he saw Arley's fat brother Delbert. His old grey pick-up truck was inching toward the exit in a long line of cars. He guessed that Delbert was going to town. His clothes would have to wait. He didn't have time to get them now. Delbert was his only chance.

"Delbert!" he yelled.

"Se:kon Darrin," Delbert said. "You gonna win today?"

"I need a ride to town," Darrin gasped. "Are you going to town right now?"

"Heh-heh-heh," Delbert emitted a squeaky laugh. "You lucked-out. I'm just on my way to get some groceries." His truck stopped. "Hop in."

Darrin ran around the truck, twisted the floppy door handle and jumped inside. He sat forward so his anklets wouldn't pinch. The pouch touched his leg and he felt it getting very warm.

"How's come you're going to town in the middle of the powwow?" Delbert let out the clutch and they bounced forward. "Did you get beat out?"

"Um, no. I'm going to show a friend my Indian clothes. I don't think he really believes I have any."

They inched out onto the highway. A serpentine of cars slowly gained speed. When they passed the turn-off to the Rez, traffic thinned out. Delbert shifted into second gear. *Brurrunngggg-ping.* The engine revved up but they lost power and coasted to the shoulder of the road.

"What was that?"

"Oh, nothin,'" Delbert smiled. "Heh-heh-heh. Sometimes she pops out of gear and I have to pop her back in." He hopped out and slammed the door. "Don't go way. Heh-heh-heh. I'll be right back."

Darrin saw Delbert climb into the bed. He grabbed a hammer and screwdriver from a tool box. He jumped from the bed and disappeared underneath the truck. Darrin's ears rung when Delbert started pounding.

Darrin's rabbit's foot was getting very hot. He gingerly removed it from the pouch. "Ahki!" It flipped beside him and it lay on the driver's seat. He worried that it might burn a hole in the upholstery.

Delbert finished pounding. He slid from beneath the truck and smiled. "There," said. "That ought to do her." He threw his tools in the back and opened the door. "What's this?" He picked up the rabbit's foot. "Is this yours?" He climbed in and studied it. He didn't seem affected by the heat. He closed the door and handed it back to Darrin.

Darrin felt *blistering* heat. He guided the rabbit's foot to the floor as Delbert started the truck.

"Here we go," Delbert said. The truck shook to life.

"I hope that took care of her," Darrin said. He also hoped Delbert didn't see him put the rabbit's foot on the floor.

After accelerating, Delbert shifted to second gear. *Thuunnk!* "There she is," he smiled. "All fixed, Heh-heh-heh."

"Does she always do that?"

"Only when I'm in a hurry." Delbert scratched his portly belly. "So I try not to be in a hurry."

Darrin looked at the speedometer. "I'll bet she could hit 80."

"You think so?"

"Nah. I take it back. This old buggy probably can't do any more than she's doin' right now."

Delbert floored the accelerator. A surge of power pushed Darrin back against his seat. They went over a roller-coaster hill and Darrin's stomach fluttered.

"I knew she could do it," Darrin said happily. "I'll bet she can even go faster."

Delbert slowed down. "Nah. I just like going fast over that little hill; it tickles my belly. Heh-heh-heh."

Darrin decided against getting him to speed up. If the gear slipped out again, he couldn't be sure that Delbert could fix it. One of Totah's old cars did the same thing. Then one day it slipped out and broke forever.

An anklet rattled when he stretched out his leg. He

clawed the rabbit's foot under the seat with his big toe. He wondered why it hadn't scorched a hole in the floorboard mat. He also wondered if Delbert's old truck would get them to L. Lafont's house in time..

tekeni yawenre (12)

A Fire In The City

Delbert stopped at Cobe's and pumped gas into the pick-up's tank. Darrin heard a rumble and saw a red hook and ladder truck roll past. Fireman clung to its side rails and the wheelman in the back waved to him. Why weren't its siren wailing or its red lights flashing? Why was it going away from the Lafont's house?

Delbert hooked the spout on the gas pump. "I'll be right out," he said.

Darrin noticed the PART-TIME HELP WANTED sign. Through the screen, he also noticed Delbert talking to Mr. Cobe. Come on, Delbert! This isn't the time to be friendly. Or to apply for the job. Let's get going.

A Fire Chief's car with its siren and roof lights off passed by. It went the same wrong direction as the fire truck. Darrin wished he knew the Lafont's phone number so he could call them. Maybe everything was okay.

Delbert hopped in, started the truck and they drove three blocks. *Brrrunngg.* "Here we go again," he said as they coasted and stopped beside a curb.

"Delbert," Darrin gasped. "Would you get mad if I ran the rest of the way? My friend only lives two blocks from here."

"No. Take off, heh-heh-heh." He hopped out and slammed the door. "I'll be goin' back home in about an hour. If you're at Cobe's I'll give you a lift."

Darrin ran down the street toward the Lafont's. He felt his bear-claw necklace pounding against his chest. A man mowing a lawn stopped and looked at him in surprise. It wasn't often that you saw a genuine Indian running down the sidewalk.

Wind hummed past Darrin's ears and drops of sweat stung his eyes. He watched a fire truck slowly pull around the corner. Firemen smudged with soot hung on to its side; their helmets tucked under their arms. They looked tired.

Darrin turned the corner and slowed to a walk. Two policemen carried off Street Closed signs while a diesel engine clattered to life. Four firemen hopped upon the running board and the last truck chugged off. Water sloshed into a sewer-grate and the air carried a sulphuric stench.

A small crowd had gathered and a woman, palms against her face, seemed hypnotized. "Tsk-tsk-tsk," she said. "Poor Lawrence. He din'nae get a chance to get much o' anythin' oot."

Darrin's moccasins got wet and squished as he crossed the street. His deer hoof anklets rattled as he approached the Lafont's charred, two-storey house. The roof had big hole in it and two walls resembled jagged piles of charcoal. Two firemen took off their yellow rain coats, wiped their brows and hobbled from the driveway.

"Where you goin' son?"

Darrin turned toward the deep voice. A big policeman stood, hands on hips; his sunglasses glinting in the sun.

"That's a nice costume you're wearing. I'm taking my son out to the powwow tomorrow."

Darrin looked at the officer's gun and his badge. "Your costume's pretty neat too," he said.

"Ha, ha, ha," the officer laughed. "It is, eh?"

"I know the guy that lives here. Do you know if he's around anywhere's?"

"There's an old fella around back."

"Could I go see him?"

"Well, I suppose so. But don't walk too close to the building and don't go inside."

"Okay, thanks." Darrin ran to the backyard. His deer hoof anklets rattled freely as he dodged debris and dirty puddles.

Blisters speckled the walls and soot blackened the windows. Mr. Lafont knelt on the ground mumbling to himself while he clipped red roses with his snippers. He had them all carefully laid out on a scrap of burlap, their prickly stems long and equal.

He bent toward a partly trampled rosebush. "My, my," he said. "They almost killed you." He looked very weary.

"Mr. Lafont?" Darrin walked toward him. "Are you okay?"

He stood up. "My, don't you look nice. I guess I won't be needing your rain dance now. Sure coulda used it half'n hour ago, though." He brushed off his pant legs.

"Is Missus Lafont okay?"

"Yeah. I had some trouble gettin' her down the porch stairs but she made it."

"Where you gonna stay?"

"I dunno, guess we'll move into an apartment now." He reached into his pocket. "I haven't had time to give it much thought." He handed Darrin a loonie.

"No, no." Darrin turned away. "I don't have no place to carry it, these clothes got no pockets. Besides, you'll need it to buy more rosebushes."

"Well here, then." He reached down and selected a rosebud. "Take this and when it blooms...you give it to your girlfriend." He snipped the stem to shorten it and handed it to Darrin. "Well, I got to go and make a phone call." He locked the snippers and rolled up the burlap. He put it under his arm and put his hand on Darrin's shoulder.

Darrin felt Mr. Lafont's hand trembling as they dodged driveway debris. He smelled the green rosebud and watched him trudge across the street. He wondered how adults always seemed to know about girlfriends. He figured it paralleled the same way he knew about things.

He put the rosebud in his pouch and started walking to Cobe's. It occurred to him that things were changing. In the blink of an eye no more Mark and no more Mr. Lafont. Why couldn't things stay the same?

"Hey! Hey kid! Need a ride back to the powwow?"

Darrin saw a shiny van pull up beside him. A big, burly man leaned toward him and talked through the passenger window. He'd never seen this man before.

"No thanks," he turned away. "I've got to meet somebody." He broke into a trot.

"Aw, come-on kid. I've got a big bag of candy in here for you."

Darrin cut across a lawn. Out of the corner of his eye he saw the van speed away. From this distance he could see Cobe's and Delbert's old pick-up wasn't there. He loped across the parking lot and leaned against a street light pole.

When Delbert arrived, he waved at Darrin, parked the truck and rushed inside. He had a sheet of paper in his hand. "I'll be right back," he winked.

Darrin climbed into the truck. He looked for the rabbit's foot, groped under the seat but couldn't find it. Good, he thought. It probably fell out the door. I'm finally rid of it forever.

Delbert climbed back inside. "I'm going to be working at Cobe's," he said. "Heh-heh-heh. I'll be pumping gas for a while but he's going to build a garage and I'm gonna be his mechanic." He reached into his pant's pocket. "Here," he handed Darrin the rabbit's foot. "I found this under the seat when I was looking for my crescent wrench."

Darrin gingerly took it. It was cold as an ice cube. He put it into his beaded pouch.

"Cobe tells me there was a fire a couple of blocks away at the Lafont place. Ain't that where your sister lives?"

"No, she don't live there anymore. She lives with us at Totah's."

"Good thing she moved." Delbert started the truck, checked for traffic and pulled out. "I'm stoppin' at home first before I go back to the powwow. You can either come with me or I can drop you off when we go by your house."

"You can drop me off. I gotta get something to eat."

After a bouncy ride home, the pick-up stopped and Darrin hopped out. He danced a two-step toward the house and looked for Totah's Ford. It wasn't in its usual place and the house seemed vacant. He broke into a trot. Good, he thought. I can raid the goodies Lisa brought with her from town. He burst into the kitchen and drew open the cloth that covered the shelf.

"Darrin!" Brenda stepped from the stairwell cradling Naomi. "What do you think you're doin?"

"I'm hungry. I didn't get nothing to eat, yet."

"Lisa got some eggs and meat. I'll make us an omelette, fry some spuds and cook you some steak." She handed Naomi to Darrin. "In the meantime, here. Make yourself useful."

Darrin took Naomi into the front room. He placed her on the floor on top of the blanket and tossed the rosebud on the window sill. He took off his Indian clothes and put on clean jeans and T-shirt. He decided to play with Naomi after she gave him a pleasant smile.

He remembered that you had to be careful when you played with babies. They didn't have very strong necks. Her eyes fascinated him. He shaded them and watched them expand and contract when he moved his hand. Suddenly, lumpy liquid-stuff started flowing from her mouth. He rushed her back to the kitchen.

A miracle of efficiency, Brenda had their meal

ready. "Just in time," she said. She took Naomi, wiped the spit-up with a tissue and sat down.

"The Lafont's house burned down today," Darrin said as he sat down at the table.

"Really? How do you know?"

Darrin loaded his plate with food. Uh-oh, he thought, me and my big mouth. Now she's gonna want to know what was I doing in town? Without her permission. He took a bite of potato.

"Well?" Brenda fixed herself a plate with one hand while holding Naomi in the other.

Maybe she all ready knows, Darrin thought. I better start my story by saying how I didn't take candy from a stranger. That'll soften her up. Then I can tell her that I *had* to go, as a result of my vision. Yeah, right. Get real. This is Brenda, not Totah. She'll never believe that I went there to warn the Lafont's about their house burning down. No way.

"Delbert told me," he lied. "He's the one gave me a ride home from the powwow." He felt his face flush. "Did you bring my clothes home?"

"No. Was the fire bad?" Brenda began eating.

"I dunno," Darrin said while he chewed. "Delbert got a job at Cobe's."

Brenda bounced Naomi on her knee. "Doodley, doodley, do," she sang, then looked at Darrin. "Did you leave your clothes at the powwow?"

"Yeah." Darrin swallowed.

"What kind of job?"

"A mechanic's job."

"Car mechanic?" Brenda took a bite of omelette.

"Yeah."

"Well that Delbert's good at fixin' cars."

Darrin cut a piece of steak. "I'll pick up my clothes tomorrow."

"You'll do nothing of the sort. You'll finish eating, hop on your bike and pick them up today. Right?"

"Right!"

Brenda waved her fork like a symphony conductor. "And you'll be home before dark, right!"

"Right!"

"You better tell Lisa the news about the fire when you get back to the powwow."

"Right!" Darrin cleaned off his plate and put his fork down.

"I'll do the dishes, now git."

Brenda held Naomi under her arm like a football while she gathered the table utensils. Darrin wondered why she didn't catch him in his lie. She always caught him before.

"I might be havin' company from the powwow and I don't want you here cluttering up the place." Brenda put the dishes in the dishpan. "So git. But get your butt back here before dark!"

Darrin ran down the hallway to the front room. So that's why she was in such a hurry, he thought. She's got company coming. He picked up the rosebud from the window sill. Good thing I didn't tell her; she didn't have time to listen anyway. He carefully removed the thorns from its stem. He pushed it into his back pocket and ran back down the hallway.

He burst out the front door and picked up his bike. He pushed its handlebars, took three strides and hopped upon the seat. He bounced across the field, hopped the ditch and peddled down the road. I'm not only going to tell Lisa, he thought, while pumping. I'm going to tell Sharla. I've got to tell somebody that the Lafont's fire was my fault.

When he peddled over Chiefswood bridge, he heard bursts of applause. The announcer was recognizing the speciality dancers and their feats of agility. In the grove beyond the dance area, he saw decorated tipis and colourful tents. He pointed his bike toward the restrooms and wiped his brow. He hopped off his bike and ran it to a stop. He leaned it against the restroom wall and went inside.

Instead of finding his clothes, he found Arley Van Peldt.

ahsen yawenre (13)

An Unusual Flight

Arley looked at him and leaned against the wall. He flicked a cigarette butt to the floor and squashed it with his boot. "Well, well." He smiled. "Look who's here."

Darrin scanned the shelf where he left his clothes. They were missing. Pretend to be afraid of your enemy, he remembered Fox advising. When he's convinced you're afraid he becomes overconfident. Then you use the element of surprise and attack. He turned and walked outside.

"Heyyy, where do you think you're going?"

Darrin felt a hand grab his arm. He shook it off and continued outside. "I lost my clothes. I've got to find them."

Arley pushed him through the doorway. "Are you saying I *stole* them? Are you accusing me of stealing?"

Darrin felt a slap and another push. He twisted his body to retain his balance. "No Arley," he said.

Arley slapped him on the forehead. "Well, I think you did!"

Darrin put up his hands for protection. Arley feinted a punch and Darrin tried to block it. He got hit in the ribs.

"What's the matter?" Arley closed his hands into fists. "Don't tell me you're afraid?" Arley's eyes became two slits. "You weren't afraid to hit me in the head with the ball, now where you?" Arley swung and missed.

"I wasn't aiming at you," Darrin said. "I was aiming where I intended to hit it."

Arley walked toward him, swung and missed. His left fist shot out to jab Darrin's chin and missed. He swung with a right cross, missed, and Darrin slapped him three times in the ribs.

Arley looked surprised. "Okay, I'm really mad now," he grunted. He ran at Darrin, swung and missed again.

Darrin let his hands dangle. He stuck out his jaw and started dancing around Arley counter clockwise. "Come on, Arley," he said. "Hit me *if* you can."

Arley swung hard as he could. Darrin ducked beneath the punch and slapped him in the belly. Arley turned and swung hard again. Off balance, he tripped and fell to the ground. He waited for Darrin to dance in front of him and lunged. He tackled Darrin and they sprawled onto the cinder pathway. Darrin saw a fist coming and twisted his head. Arley's wallop barely missed his ear. It slammed the cinders.

"Oww," Arley said. He grabbed his hand and shook it.

Darrin saw two meaty hands grab Arley's shoulders and lift him off. "That's enough!" a big man said.

Darrin jumped to his feet and glanced around. Arley gasped for breath, doubled over and held his bruised hand. His face wrinkled in pain. Several people had seen the scuffle but Darrin only recognized one of the faces. It was Sharla.

She stood with her arms hugging a grocery bag. She walked toward Darrin and the fringes of her buckskin dress swayed. Arley started coughing and ran off toward the crafts midway.

"Hi Sharla," Darrin said emitting a toothy grin.

"You know fighting is a weakness, not a strength." She flashed the Eagle eye. "You had to be weak, didn't you?"

"I wasn't fighting," Darrin suppressed a laugh. "I was just dodging."

"I looked everywhere for you when I finished my speciality dance. All I could find were these." She tossed the grocery bag to him. "Somebody threw them out of the restrooms. They were scattered all over," she said, dropping her eyes. "I put them in that paper grocery bag for you."

Darrin pretended to inspect his clothes. Without realizing it, he leaned forward and kissed her forehead. Sharla turned away in surprise and looked at him. Full of confidence, he tried to kiss her again.

Sharla turned her back to him and started walking away. "I've got to go to my campsite," she said. "I've got to get my bathing cap; I'm going for a swim."

"Come back, Sharla." Darrin fumbled for the rosebud.

"I'm glad you didn't get hurt this time." She looked back over her shoulder at him. "I'm *not* glad you chose to be rude to my Aunty Karen."

Darrin squeezed the grocery bag in disgust. He watched her fringes swish as she walked away. He took the rosebud from his pocket but realized he missed the moment. Women, he thought. No matter what I do its wrong.

He walked back to the restrooms and stuffed the rosebud into his back pocket. He held the grocery bag like a football and hopped upon his bike. He sulked because he couldn't celebrate his victory with Sharla. He felt a need to tell her everything.

Pedaling home, he went beneath Chiefswood bridge to admire a rippling, magenta sunset. Drawn to the water like a bug to a light bulb, he decided to skip stones. He lay the grocery bag on the ground and positioned the back wheel on it for weight.

He collected flat stones on his way to the water. With a good stone, he could usually get eight skips. Tonight he fantasized twenty; he was on a roll.

By the fifth throw he managed eleven skips. Power boats pulled water skiers who were in a frenzy to beat the darkness. He watched them buzz under the bridge and disappear past the powwow grounds. Waves lapped against his sneakers. He sat down on a log to wait for the waves to stop. You couldn't go for a twenty under these conditions.

He pondered the significance of his dreams. He heard that dreams could be magical. He wondered if anybody could know whether they were or not. What made a dream good? What made one bad? Was the Lafont dream bad? He took out the rosebud to sniff it. It had become flattened and he squeezed it back into shape. He dunked it into the water to rinse pocket fuzz and dirt off it.

Suddenly, he heard a loud, flute-like song. It seemed like an echo and came from beneath a stand of pine trees across the river. Its notes were bright and clear; a melody like no other. He heard three, four, five choruses of a beautiful up and down rendition. The water seemed to amplify its volume. He tried to focus on the source of the beautiful song. He strained his eyes to look beneath the pine's bottom branches but saw nothing. A powerboat slapped through the water and the singing stopped.

He stroked the rosebud and slid it back into his pocket. It was getting dark and he had to leave. He gave one last try for a twenty but the disturbed water would only yield a nine. He picked up his bike, tucked the grocery bag under an arm and tugged it to the road. He hopped on the seat and began his trek home. His sore ankle rubbed against the chain guard.

"Ahki," he said. He kicked at the chain guard with his heel, missed, and almost fell off. He was getting sick of riding this old bike.

When he arrived at home it was still dusk. Holding the grocery bag tightly, he hopped off, in side-saddle fashion. The bike crashed against the house. He could see Brenda's silhouette in the kitchen window and ran inside. He wanted to tell her about the payoff with Arley.

"There's a couple of scones in the pie pan on the stove," Brenda said. "What's in the bag?"

"My clothes. Sharla found them and put them in this bag."

"That was nice of her. Well, dump 'em in the laundry and fold up that grocery bag...you know where it goes, right?"

"Right!"

"We saved three scones for you."

"I'm not very hungry." Darrin held the grocery bag over his head as if displaying the Heavyweight Championship Belt. He decided not to tell her about confronting Arley; he feared an I-told-you-so. He dumped the clothes into a hamper and handed Brenda the grocery bag.

"Well, of course you're not hungry. I remember what it's like to be living on *love*."

There she goes again, Darrin thought. What do you have to do to get your message across to adults?

"I am not living on love," Darrin said. He walked to the stove. "See?" He held up a scone and took a big bite. "I am now *eating* this scone."

"What happened? You and Sharla have a lover's quarrel?"

"No." Darrin made a chomping noise. "She doesn't like me anymore and I don't like her anymore."

"Don't tell me you tried to kiss her," Brenda smiled.

There she goes again Darrin thought. How does she always know these things?

"She wouldn't let me."

"She wouldn't let you?"

"Yeah. It's no big deal. I kissed her on the forehead and tried to kiss her on the lips but she wouldn't let me."

Brenda laughed. "Maybe Sharla wanted you to kiss her on the lips in the first place."

Darrin walked down the hallway and out onto the porch. He fell on the car seat and slumped. Crickets were singing and he watched fireflies blinking. Normally he would have hunted them but he didn't feel like chasing anything tonight.

He finished the scone and climbed under the Army blanket. He took out the rosebud and wished he would have given it to Sharla. Women always went ga-ga over flowers. He wondered why she seemed so special.

Suddenly, he saw himself flying! He felt weightless as a balloon as his body glided and dipped over the countryside. To steer, he didn't have to do anything; just think or twist himself. A hawk looked at him as if in disbelief. Darrin banked and swooped toward the river below. He puzzled at his agility and the quietness of the ride. The wind made his eyes feel scratchy and he squinted. He watched power boats and water skiers skimming on top of the river.

He zipped over the water and tried to touch his chin. Suddenly, a big tree appeared from nowhere. He zoomed straight up as if an after-burner had kicked in; his heart felt like it was in his mouth. He heard the big drum beating and saw the powwow grounds. He decided to check it out. He peeled off and flew past the arbour causing its leaves to rustle. Nobody saw him.

He sped toward Chiefswood bridge, went under it and climbed toward the sun. He looked over his shoulder and saw a red power boat. It made a wide arc and a woman skier whipped around until she was almost even with the boat's stern. The driver turned in the opposite direction to keep the towline taught. This prevented the skier from loosing speed and sinking.

Darrin saw something bobbing in the water in front of them. He stopped and hovered. It looked like a beach ball. As it slowly revolved, it became clear that it was somebody's face. He recognized Sharla's face!

The driver looked back at the skier and didn't see the ball. At this altitude, Darrin couldn't reach Sharla in time. He tried to yell to her. "Herrmmff...herrmmff!"

The power boat hit the yellow ball with a sickening thud. Blood splashed across the water. An inkblot of red burbled in the boat's wake as it sped past. The ball had disappeared. "Herrmmff!"

Darrin sat up. Sweat poured from his forehead and hands.

kayeli yawenre (14)

Taking Charge

At breakfast, Darrin pondered his strange dream. No wonder birds sing all the time, its such fun to fly. Wonder if I'll be able to fly tonight? This time I'm not going near the river. Instead, I'll go the other way; toward Lake Erie. He took a spoonful of mush.

"Good thing you're up so early," Brenda said. She spread a blanket on the kitchen floor. "You'll have to watch Naomi while Lisa and I pick potatoes. Unless you want to pick them?"

"No, no," Darrin swallowed. "I'll watch Naomi. But if she has an accident, I'm bringing her right out to youse."

"Good. And you can do the dishes, right?"

"Right!"

They carefully placed Naomi on the blanket and took a burlap sack from the wall. Brenda playfully tried to pull it over Lisa's head as they ran outside.

Darrin finished washing the dishes. He went outside to toss the dishwater and saw Brenda and Lisa playing. They were giggling and throwing dirt clots and potatoes at each other. He had never seen Lisa having so much fun. When Mark was around, she always seemed so serious.

Darrin put the dishpan away. Naomi swung her arms and kicked her legs in toothless glee. Hard to image that sweet, innocent little kid is going to turn into one of *them*, Darrin thought. He smoothed her blanket. Wonder if she'll grow up to be as pleasant as Sharla?

Sharla! He saw the image of her smiling face on the yellow beach ball. He heard laughter from outside. No sense telling those two hyenas about my odd dream, he thought. They'll just laugh at me. I suppose I should tell Sharla about it. If I see her today at the powwow. No sense telling Naomi. She wouldn't understand it anyway.

"What should I do, Naomi?" He wiped off her chin slobbers with the dishtowel.

"What're you doing?" Brenda burst through the door ahead of Lisa. "You shouldn't wipe her with the dish towel." She knelt down and picked up Naomi. "It's too rough on her sensitive, new skin."

"Here you go," said Lisa. She handed the half full sack to Darrin.

"Since you're so good at washing people's faces, you can wash the potatoes and halve them, right?"

"Wrong." Darrin hooked the dish towel on its nail.

"You have to. I'm going to make potato soup for lunch."

"I can't." Darrin started for the front room. "I've got to bead my belt for the powwow," he lied.

"That's strange," Brenda said. "When I put your belt away I didn't notice *anything* wrong with it. I even checked to make sure the new beads you put on didn't loosen up."

Darrin felt his face flush. She got me again, he thought. Now what am I gonna do? I better tell her that I have to go to the powwow to see Sharla.

"I know what your problem is," Brenda smiled. "You want to git to the powwow to see Sharla."

Darrin's face brightened. "Yeah, that's it. I gotta get to the powwow to see Sharla. It's a matter of life and death. How did you know?"

"Ha, ha, ha," Lisa laughed. "Now it's a matter of life and death, eh?" She lay the sack at his feet.

"You can't get a ride to the powwow anyways. Totah left for a Longhouse meeting this morning and he won't be back until tomorrow." Brenda rubbed noses with Naomi. "Unless you ride your bike."

"I can't carry my dance stuff if I ride my bike." Darrin picked up the sack. "I'm not pedalling to the powwow on that crummy bike with my Indian clothes on. The feathers'll get wrecked."

"You could put them in one of my hat boxes," Lisa said. "Then you could carry everything."

Darrin removed a saucepan from its nail and picked up the burlap sack. "Never mind," he said. He dragged the sack out the doorway. "Good thing I'm not competing today."

He walked to the stump and lay the pan and sack beside it. He got the pail, went to the well and threw it in. The pail's splash sent waves of water against the well wall. Shar-la, Shar-la the echoes seemed to say. He decided to make another attempt to confide in Sharla. He had to deliver the rosebud to her. It was a promise he owed to Mr. Lafont. He'd use it to introduce his dilemma.

He went back to the stump and poured water into the pan. After skinning one potato with his thumbs, a sense of urgency gripped him. He knew something was going to happen yet he couldn't be sure what it was.

He threw the potato into the sack and ran back inside the house. "Here," he said to Lisa. "I've got to go."

"That was fast," Lisa said. "Where are you going?"

He bolted outside. "I've got to get to the powwow. Fast!"

He ran toward his bike and searched his pockets. The rosebud wasn't in any of them. Where did he put it? He ran around to the front porch and climbed its railing. He picked up the Army blanket and shook it. Where could it be? He groped under the car seat.

An empty feeling plunged to his stomach. He jumped off the porch and scampered beneath it. He saw something pink. It was the rosebud and it had begun to unfold. Why was it pink? All of Lafont's other roses had been red. He stroked its velvet smoothness. He crawled out from under the porch. He tucked it into his hip pocket and grabbed his bicycle.

He ran beside it and plopped into its seat like a rodeo rider. He cut across the field and jumped the ditch. He heard the gravel crunch when he landed. Tires bounced and the bike groaned as he stood up to pump. *Skeeaa-skeeaa-skeeaa* the chain rubbed. Wind pushed against his body and hummed in his ears.

He went down the hill and almost fell off taking the turn at the river. He passed Truman Cloud's house but didn't even have time to wave. *Up-down, up-down, up-down.* He wiped his brow and felt his muscles tighten. He tried to breathe in rhythm with his pedalling. It didn't work.

He saw Chiefswood bridge and rode to the middle of it. He stopped and gasped for air. His heart pounded like the big drum at the powwow. His face felt hot and puffy. He checked the river for power boats. There were none. He sighed with relief. All he heard were campsite murmurs. He patted the rosebud to make sure it was still there. It felt warm.

He rode past the arbour toward the campsites. I have to tell Sharla about her dream, he convinced himself. I don't want to make another mistake like I did with the Lafont's. He recognized Aunty Karen and dragged his feet to stop.

"Se:kon Darrin," she said. "Are you going to dance today?"

"No," Darrin said. He was grateful that she didn't seem mad at him. "Where's Sharla?"

"She went down to the river for a quick swim before Grand Entry starts. She should be finished any minute now."

"Which way?"

"Over that way," she pointed toward a boat dock.

"Can I leave my bike here?"

"Sure, go ahead. Nobody owns the woods."

Hopping from the bike, his pants tightened against his leg. He felt heat coming from the pocket that held the rosebud. "I'll be back for it later," he said, leaning the bike against a tree.

He walked through the woods toward the water. When he reached the dock, he watched two men unload a red boat from a trailer. A woman sat on the edge wearing water skis. She was tying a knot in a yellow, nylon towrope. Darrin looked up and down the river but couldn't see Sharla anywhere. He looked toward the arbour but she wasn't there either.

He sat on the dock and dangled his legs. Water spiders skittered among the dock pilings. One of the men swore and quickly began sucking his finger. They pushed the boat into the water. He took the rosebud from his pocket to look at it. It felt warmer than his body heat; it seemed to be getting hot!

A motor buzzed to life and the boat swung around pulling its towline tight. It accelerated and in an instant the woman was skimming along behind the boat. Someday I'm going to give water-skiing a try, Darrin thought. That looks like fun.

A tail of white water seemed to chase the boat. The rosebud got hotter and Darrin put it on a plank beside him. He wondered why it was getting so hot. Just like his rabbit's foot.

From the corner of his eye, he saw a yellow bathing cap shoot out of the water. He heard the red boat's motor lower its pitch. The boat made a wide arc.

Inside the yellow bathing cap he saw Sharla's shiny face. "Sharla!" He jumped to his feet and waved his arms. "Sharla!" He heard the red boat's motor scream to full throttle.

"Sharla!" He tore off his sneakers and dove into the river. He scooped and kicked as hard and as fast as he could. "Sharla!" She was four metres away.

Sharla smiled and bobbed like a float on a fishing line. Darrin thrashed water as fast as he could. He saw the boat bearing down on her; its driver still watching the skier behind him.

He heard somebody from shore scream. He lunged and gave his hardest frog kick. He snagged the bottom of her bathing suit and jackknifed his body. He yanked her under just as the boat passed over. A white, swirling whirlpool from the propeller blades barely missed his knee.

He came to the surface gasping for air. He put a finger in his ear and popped it while he shook his head. He had water inside it and everything sounded like an echo. He heard the boat cut its engine and slowly turn toward them.

Sharla popped to the surface and tried to slap him. "You did that on purpose!" She spat a mouthful of water in his face.

Darrin wiped off his face. "What?"

"Pull my bathing suit off! That's what!"

Darrin dodged her bobbing slaps.He heard the boat's motor shut off and saw it drifting toward them.

"Are you kids all right?" A woman held her cheeks. "Oh, God, please tell us you're all right!"

"We're all right." Darrin dog paddled furiously. "At least I am."

"That sure was a courageous thing you did young

man," the woman skier said. "I saw the whole thing from behind the boat."

"I, um, we're okay."

The engine started up and the boat slowly burbled away. "That sure was an adult thing to do young man!" The driver flashed a two thumbs-up sign.

Sharla dog paddled and looked at him. "You saved my life, didn't you?"

"Um, not really." Darrin gazed straight into her brown eyes. "Let's just say a little bird..."

"Huh? I can't hear you, wait a minute." She reached under her bathing cap and removed an ear plug from each ear. "There. Now I can hear again. What did you say?"

"I, um, I said not really."

"No, I mean about the bird. Didn't you say something about a little bird?"

Darrin thought about the Hermit Thrush story. The littlest bird got the Creator's best song. He shares it because it's sacred and he only sings in secret. He has to be wary of others to protect it. He doesn't brag about his gift or use it to show off.

"Let's just say a Hermit Thrush told me," Darrin said.

"A Hermit Thrush? What's a Hermit Thrush?"

"Maybe I'll tell you someday...*if* you're lucky."

"An' maybe I'll give you a kiss someday *if* you're lucky."

"Huh?"

Sharla took a deep breath and exhaled. "Well anyway I'm glad you saved my life." She cupped her hand and pushed water in his face. "Okay, Mr. Hermit Thrush." She turned and swam away. "Race you back to the dock."

Darrin wiped his face. "I'm too tired to race," he kicked his legs and started after her.

Sharla got to the dock first. She climbed out of the water, pulled off her bathing cap and fluffed her long, black hair. "I've got to get ready for Grand Entry," she gasped. "Are you dancing today?"

Darrin pulled up from the water. "You *could* help me up, you know."

"Okay." She bent over and extended her hand. "Well, come on then."

He took her hand and she pulled him up. Suddenly, she twisted it free. Darrin fell off the dock backwards. *Splash!* By the time he swam back, he saw Sharla skipping from the dock onto the bank. She stopped to wave at him and he heard her giggle.

He saw the rosebud still lying on the plank. He knew there wouldn't be any heat coming from it now, so he picked it up. He realized it wasn't the rabbit's foot or the rosebud that had the power. It was him. He had a powerful gift just like the Hermit Thrush.

He felt a feeling of relief followed by a rush of joy.

Maybe having the sweetest of all songs wouldn't be so bad after all, he mused. It sure came in handy today.

Sharla started jogging toward her campsite.

"Sharla!" He held up the limp rosebud. "Sharla!" He started to run after her. "Wait up! I've got this pink rose for you. It's special. It's the only pink one Mr. Lafont ever had."

He thought about tackling her but changed his mind. After all she did say kiss, didn't she? He smelled the rosebud. Even though it was shabby, it still gave off fragrance. Sharla would find it suitable because it was the thought that counted. What something cost didn't matter. It was the meaning. He learned that lesson from Lisa.

Darrin ran hard as he could. He'd catch up to her, give her the pink rosebud and collect his kiss. Somehow, he just *knew* it.

THE END

Author Richard G. Green was born in Ohsweken at Lady Willingdon hospital in Grand River Territory. He went to school and grew up in Ontario province and New York state. He began studying writing in the late '60s and has contributed short stories, articles and cartoons to Onkwehonwe publications and literature anthologies in Canada and United States. In 1994 he published a collection of short stories. This is his first book about young people. He lives on the Six Nations Reserve where he creates writings for the North American Indian media.

Cover illustrator Raymond Skye has worked diligently to distinguish himself as an artist. He studied at Mohawk College in Hamilton, Ontario and has chosen the drawing media and its techniques to express himself. An appreciation for wildlife, portraiture, architecture and still life give him a profusion of imagery. He juxtaposes and blends reality with illusion to present his passion for romance and history. He enjoys the challenges of art but his biggest challenge is finding time to paint as often as he desires.